BYRON'S LANE

A NOVEL

BYRON'S LANE

A NOVEL

WALLACE ROGERS

LANGDON STREET PRESS

Minneapolis, MN

Langdon Street Press
212 3rd Avenue North, Suite 290
Minneapolis, MN 55401
612.455.2293
www.langdonstreetpress.com

ISBN-13: 978-1-62652-131-5
LCCN: 2013939312

Distributed by Itasca Books

Cover Design by Alan Pranke
Typeset by Jenni Wheeler

Printed in the United States of America

"Lord Byron was nothing if not the prototype of the conflicted Romantic hero. His persona has influenced artists possibly more than his art itself. His work was a synthesis of medieval and classical inspiration with a modern sensibility. When he read his poetry, people listened."

Meg Wise-Lawrence, *The Germ*

PROLOGUE

Part of him died in Iraq. The experience shrunk him. It killed his aura of innocence. It sapped his exuberance. It ended his quest to make the world a better place than it was when he became part of it.

I knew we had lost the best of Adams when he coldly described to me what happened in Samarra—two weeks before he left Iraq, six weeks after his friends were assassinated in Mosul.

Mosul and Samarra channeled his slide into the Waters of Lethe. Because both events occurred months after the national news media had packed up and left Iraq, and weeks before America's military presence there evaporated, we heard nothing about them. Our fickle attention had turned to other places in the world and more pressing matters back in the States.

*

Jonathan Adams spent eight months in Iraq, working as a civilian contractor on an American foreign aid project. The day trip to Samarra was his last scheduled field assignment. He was riding in a four-vehicle military convoy when it stopped alongside a dusty traffic circle next to Samarra's Malwiya Minaret, a mile from the municipal building he had just toured. A TV reporter recently arrived from Scranton, Pennsylvania, to cover its Army Reserve civil affairs battalion's last two weeks on the job and their trip back to Scranton, wanted to use the landmark as a backdrop for an interview with the battalion's ranking officer—a bookish, bespectacled forty-year-old lieutenant colonel. Everybody except two turret gunners and one of the drivers had left their vehicles. They were gathered around the Humvees, snacking on candy bars and sunflower seeds, smoking cigarettes, talking about going home. The reporter and his cameraman were busy setting up for the interview.

A teenage boy emerged from a group of Iraqi men huddled around a card table full of bootleg videos. The video stand was a football field's length away from where the convoy had stopped. The boy joined three women in burkas with two small children in hand as they walked along the shoulder of the traffic circle. The women and children turned down a side street; the boy continued to walk toward the Americans.

He was less than ten yards away when he shouted, "Allahu Akbar!" He clenched his teeth and pushed a button on a small black plastic garage door opener concealed in the palm of his right hand.

The boy looked bewildered when nothing happened. His forehead furrowed. His mouth dropped open. A second lieutenant pulled his handgun out of his shoulder holster and shot him in the head. The boy's knees buckled, and he crumpled like a collapsing house of cards. Blood pulsing from the hole in his forehead formed an expanding sticky purple circle on the hot black asphalt. Silence followed the sharp, crisp sound of the single gun shot.

The stillness shattered when someone in uniform— Adams didn't notice who—shouted: "Let's go, gentlemen! Return to your vehicles! Mount up now!"

Everybody scrambled back into the Humvees. Four turret gunners cocked their .50-caliber machine guns. Everyone was quickly accounted for by the drivers, who spoke to each other on their headsets loud enough for Adams to hear from the backseat. The whole process hardly took a minute.

The convoy lurched through the roundabout and drove quickly out of town. In a controlled rush, they speeded toward a small, abandoned, fortified outpost, just off the Mosul-to-Baghdad highway that skirted Samarra on its west side.

Forty minutes later, beside the sand-scarred concrete blast walls that partially surrounded the place, and guarded by a platoon of infantry just arrived by helicopter, the Channel 6 news team from Scranton, Pennsylvania, nervously set up its camera again. The lieutenant colonel asked the reporter to make no mention in his broadcast about what had happened on the traffic circle. The colonel did his interview, and the detachment's majors, lieutenants, sergeants, and E-4s taped Thanksgiving Day greetings to friends and relatives back home. Some were shown on the six o'clock news that night. The partially rebuilt dome of Samarra's Askariya Shrine was the backdrop now, ten kilometers off in the distance.

The second lieutenant who shot the boy didn't do an interview. He sat alone on the ground, leaning against a T-wall, staring off into the desert, smoking cigarettes one after another.

The profound impression the incident made on Jonathan Adams was consummate awe. He marveled at how the movement from the shadows of the Malwiya Minaret to the FOB safe place had been executed, how their extraction from the situation on the traffic circle unfolded exactly according to the "In Case Something Happens" plan the major and first sergeant in charge of the mission described in the 0-900 briefing, before Adams was given his seat assignment and the convoy left division headquarters.

When he called me from Minnesota and told me all this on the telephone, less than two weeks after it happened, Adams made no mention of what it feels like to be a millisecond away from being blown up, or seeing someone ten feet away from you get shot in the head.

Six weeks before the Samarra incident, in Mosul, all the warm and soft parts of Jonathan Adams ossified and grew stone cold. By the time Samarra happened, he'd become numb and indifferent.

*

When I was young, my father gave me some advice: "Watch and learn," he'd said. Before I explain what happened in Mosul, know that I am a trained observer.

It's hardly a rare talent. My generation has sprouted so many like me that this description could be written on our collective tombstone in thirty or forty years, when the last of us are finally dead and buried. But I have a natural aptitude for it.

Mine is the first generation that's learned life's lessons by watching thousands of hours of television. In the process, most of us have evolved finely-tuned voyeuristic tendencies, an enhanced, detached curiosity, and a self-absorbed interest in the misfortunes of others. These are reinforced in people like me who've read hundreds of books and watched a multitude of movies. As much as I want it to be otherwise, television, books, and movies provide the lens through which I interpret almost everything I see and experience.

Jonathan Adams is the only one I know of our generation who spent most of his time feeling, doing, and thinking instead of watching. Fueled by hope and faith, he was constantly chasing possibilities. In the meantime, while I occasionally stopped to watch the world go by and draw some judgment about it, cynicism and doubt caught up to me.

Iraq made Adams like the rest of us.

*

Movies, books, and television taught me that when your telephone rings in the middle of the night, what happens after you pick up is almost always disturbing.

I vividly recall his frantic first words. They were draped in anxiety and knocked me awake.

"I met with them for our morning briefing in the conference room an hour ago. Hind gave her camera to Hassan. He took a picture of the four of us. I'm looking at it now. She e-mailed the picture to me just before they left. All three of them are dead, Tom."

His sentences tumbled over each other and crashed against my ears, like surging waves against a harbor break wall.

"It happened because I'm here in Iraq. I have no business being in Iraq. I'm the one who should be dead. I'm the only one alive in this picture."

It was unlike any exchange we've had before or since. I could hear his sobs five thousand miles away.

He took a deep breath.

"If they didn't work for me, Tom, they'd be home tonight with their families. I asked them to go to a fucking senseless meeting for me—so that what I'm doing here would have an Iraqi face to it. What did these kids die for?"

His voice grew halting. His latest words, more

softly spoken, were barely able to penetrate his grief and his guilt—so fresh, so stifling—apparent to me half the world away.

"I sent them off to do things I was sure should be done—to make this mess we've made of Iraq have a happy Hollywood ending. I convinced them that what we were trying to do was empowering. I told them that democracy is life-changing." He paused. "I got part of it right, didn't I, Tom? Their families' lives were surely changed today, weren't they?"

His words came fast, falling over one another. "I was so damn sure that everybody everywhere wanted freedom to hope, freedom to dream, freedom from fear—the same freedoms we enjoy." He paused. "That's bullshit, Tom. It took the slaughter of three extraordinary people to make me realize that. How could I have been so stupid and arrogant?"

He breathed heavily. Then his words burst into the telephone. "I was so sure the Iraqis wanted this, in spite of a hundred things a blind man could have seen going on all around me. I was so sure that I risked the lives of three beautiful people to try to make it the way I thought it ought to be. What have I done? What do I say to their families?"

I was sharply awake now. Adams's sobs faded in

and out of his cell phone. The transmission of his words from so far away and the unchecked emotion that attended them dispersed in my ear, went dead for half seconds, and then gathered and gushed, sharply audible again. My free hand scrambled over the nightstand and found a switch beneath the lampshade. As I turned on the light, I kicked back the blanket that covered me and swung my feet to the floor. What I wanted to say was catching up to what he was telling me.

"Adams, are you okay? Are you safe? Tell me what happened."

The pause that followed was long enough to make me ask Adams if he was still there. I heard him swallow.

"They were in my car. It happened right after they drove out of the compound, three blocks from here. The car was hit by an RPG. They died an awful, horrible way, Tom."

There was silence in my bedroom, punctured by faint, soft sobs that dripped through my handset's earpiece. "I killed them—as sure as the son-of-a-bitch who fired the thing."

Another pause. I had nothing to say to fill the intermittent silence. I should have said something comforting—something to challenge his damning assertion that he was the reason his friends had died.

But Adams's words and the bone-chilling emotion that accompanied them left me speechless.

Killed, he told me, were his translator, his office manager, and his project coordinator. They were seated in the back of the car, the part penetrated by the rocket-propelled grenade; three Iraqi women, all in their late twenties, two of them young wives and mothers, on their way to an insignificant lunchtime meeting.

"When I heard the explosion, I ran outside," he said.

He saw a plume of smoke—a silver-changing–to-gray-changing-to-black billowing column of smoke. Tiny black specks rained down on his head and shoulders as he stood a few feet beyond the threshold of his building's front door. Adams knew what had happened. The few guards still standing at the compound's checkpoint when he burst through the gate were unable to stop him. He ran down the street, toward awful silence that turned into plaintive whimpers that grew into screams and long, mournful wails.

"When I got there, I helped pull my bodyguard out of the car's front seat. The front half of the car was detached from the back half. The driver had opened his door and was wandering around the wreckage, holding his ears. There was blood leaking from the places where his hands were pressed. I heard short bursts of gunfire."

He told me he would never forget the sight of the smoldering carnage. He couldn't bear to glance inside the burning hulk that had been his white Toyota. He'd never forget the smell.

I was helpless, eight time zones away.

"Please hang on, Tom. My security chief is standing in the doorway. He wants to tell me something. I'll be back in a minute or two." Sobs strangely accompanied his explanation for the interruption and punctuated his request. He likely really needed time to pull himself together. I reached over to the nightstand and pushed a button on the answering machine to activate the speakerphone. I rose from the bed and walked a few feet to my desk—in front of the bedroom window. I turned on my laptop computer and opened the last e-mail I had received from Adams. Attached to it was a picture.

The picture was of Adams and his staff. They were posed in the walled courtyard outside his office. They had arranged themselves in two rows—eight of them standing, five of them kneeling. It was easy to pick out Adams's women. He was in the middle of the back row, and they stood on either side of him. Two of the three had their arms folded in front of them, just like he did. A lump rose in my throat. As I stared at the picture, my mind tumbled back to the week before he left for Iraq, four lifetimes ago.

Adams had signed a contract with the State Department. He was going to Iraq to help them organize local governments so they could provide the basic services that cities provide people in the United States. In the process of showing them how to efficiently collect and get rid of their garbage, he would teach democracy to a new crop of community leaders and politicians who were only theoretically aware of its components. Jonathan Adams was qualified to spread the democracy gospel; he fervently believed in its principles and the benefits of good governance.

Adams had hastily arranged a leave of absence from the University of Minnesota; he temporarily abandoned his seat in the Minnesota State Senate, its spring session having just concluded. He managed his escape from Minnesota so quickly that the local media wasn't aware of his plans until after he had left the country.

When he passed through New York, my friend confided to me over lunch that one of the reasons he needed to go to Iraq was because he was ashamed he had kept his hand down the last time his country involved itself in a war he couldn't support. His easy avoidance of our generation's war was owed to a college deferment and a high draft lottery number. His place in Vietnam was unfairly filled, he said, by some poor bastard who had neither.

Born in his pre-teenage Kennedy years, Adams's civic commitment was unbridled. He single-mindedly began his preparation for a life in the public sector in junior high. He improved and refined his capabilities as his career in politics played out.

I stared at the picture. I ran my finger down Adams's image and shook my head. The sense of hope he sprinkled on anyone who'd listen to him and the dreams he pursued were always too fragile a foundation on which to build a body of work and a lifetime of achievement. There's a good reason we measure success in America these days by what we accumulate rather than how many lives we've influenced. Changing someone's life in a positive way is an accomplishment impossible to quantify. Such achievement fits nowhere inside a contemporary portrait of an America framed by measurable outcomes.

For the first time in fifty years—as long as I had known him—it was apparent that Adams was without a bearing, a heading, a plan, a compass. He was far from home, in an unfamiliar place, drowning in a culture he didn't understand and couldn't accommodate, or tolerate, anymore. He had wandered, uninvited, into the middle of a civilization that seemed to be driven by political and spiritual leaders who wanted to burn the place down so it might rise from the ashes and flourish as it had during Muslim's glory years, more than a millennium ago.

Adams's voice on the speakerphone pierced the bedroom and snapped my attention away from the picture. I shut down the computer, returned to my bedside, and picked up the telephone.

"If all this weren't so fucking bloody and horrific, so utterly, contemptibly wasteful and backward, all it would be is absurd. We could ignore it—if we could find a better way to fuel our cars and make things out of plastic. Goddamn oil! We should build a wall around this wasteland and let them simmer and stew in their hate for modernity, their fifteen-hundred-year religious feuds, and their prejudice against women—out of sight and out of mind."

I had never heard Jonathan Adams talk like this. He scared me. He disappointed me. But I understood what drove his words. I instantly forgave him.

"I need to come home, Tom, before my fractured beliefs get someone else killed."

I asked if there was anything I could do to help facilitate his departure. I could travel from New York to Minneapolis on a day's notice, meet him at the airport when he returned, and spend his first week at home with him.

Recovering some of his familiar self, he told me that wouldn't be necessary. He had responsibilities to which he had to attend in Iraq, loose ends he had to tie together before he could leave. He wasn't sure how long these obligations might take. He said he would come home as soon as they were handled.

I thought Adams was referring to the time he needed to spend with his staff and his women's families to help them mourn their shared loss. He probably required a few weeks to pass his project on to a new program manager. I've since learned that most of the rest of Adams's time in Iraq was spent directing what he later called "an appropriate response" to what had happened to his friends.

*

After I hung up the phone, I picked a book up from the floor that I'd been reading before I'd fallen asleep. The thick black-and-brown-jacketed book was a biography of John Kennedy. I carried it down the hallway and through my darkened living room, barely illuminated by a streetlight beyond the large front window. I laid the book on the desk in my study.

Like most people who were alive when it happened, I remember exactly where I was when I first heard the news.

It was early Friday afternoon—a wet, gray day. I had gym class on Mondays, Wednesdays, and Fridays, right after lunch. I spent lunch hour that Friday unable to eat, sick to my stomach. Before English class, someone fresh from first-period gym told me that Mr. Schilling had brought the mats, the vault, and the parallel bars out of the storage room. The dreaded inevitability of having to face tumbling and gymnastics three times a week for at least a month stared me in the face, then punched me in the gut.

I was wearing white gym shorts, a white crewneck Hanes T-shirt, cotton Wigwam socks, and black Converse Chuck Taylor All-Star basketball sneakers. I was in the school's gymnasium, standing at the south end of the basketball court, in the middle of a line of ten freshmen boys dressed exactly like me, shivering. I was hoping no one noticed. Maplewood's school superintendent waded as far into Ohio's autumn as possible before he ordered the heat turned on in all the school buildings. I convinced myself that my shaking was as likely caused by low room temperature as it was by naked fear.

Twenty feet in front of us, lying on his back, was Mike O'Brien. He was staring apprehensively in my direction between his bent knees. I was third in line. In less than twenty seconds I would have to run at O'Brien and somersault over him, my extended arms pushing off his knees as he helped my inverted body safely clear the place where his head lay on the cold blue mat. I had no talent for tumbling. My ineptitude was infinitely compounded by stark memories of spectacular failures, having never accomplished the handspring somersault since I was first challenged to try one as a seventh grader.

Raising his head off the mat, O'Brien's legs framed his darting eyes as he looked nervously ahead. He knew my record. Everyone did. What was about to happen would look like newsreel footage of a Japanese kamikaze attack on a U.S. Navy aircraft carrier. The joints in my knees and elbows were turning to goo as I approached the front of the line.

But profound embarrassment and likely injury were postponed that gray, damp Friday. A clap of thunderous static from deep inside the school's intercom system burst through two meshed boxes hanging on the wall behind us, next to the scoreboard. The noise stopped everything. It was followed by the assistant principal's tap on his microphone to make sure it was working. We reacted like people whose names had been shouted out in a crowd. All of our attention instinctively turned to the source of the sound.

Mr. Marcus's voice followed farther behind the crackle and the tap than it usually did. His six words echoed throughout the cavernous gym: "Students: President Kennedy has been assassinated."

His short announcement, made haltingly, with a never-before-heard twinge of emotion, rippled through the vacant space around me, then retreated back through the public address system. The incessant waves of a national radio news broadcast followed, and filled our classrooms the rest of the school day.

We stood in our lines for a while, listening to CBS radio, dumbly staring at the olive-green block wall behind us and the black electric scoreboard and the two speakers attached to it. No one in the gym spoke for a very long time. Silence was finally broken when Coach Schilling told us to go back into the locker room and change. Gym class was over.

We shuffled, uncharacteristically quiet, through sixth, seventh, and eighth periods. The piped-in radio provided the day's lesson in all of our remaining classes. Teachers sat, heads bowed, on the front corners of their desks. As disturbing as the news was, it was almost as unsettling to watch the adults around us react to it. They were stunned, off-kilter—unable to tell us how to absorb the information that dumped down upon us from the wooden speakers above the green chalkboards in each of our classrooms.

At half past three the last bell rang. I had twenty minutes to get my jacket and gym bag from my locker and collect whatever else I needed to take home, go out into what was left of an overcast November afternoon, and board yellow bus Number 8 for a four-mile ride home to Byron's Lane. Mr. Dawkins, our bus driver, took no notice of me as I climbed the two steps inside the bus's opened accordion door. His eyes were staring at his lap as he listened to a small transistor radio propped up on the sill of the open vent window.

Jonathan Adams already occupied half of our bench seat near the back of the bus. The green vinyl felt colder than usual as I slid in next to him, and he moved away from me, hard against the side of the bus.

During the ride home, speaking in muffled voices like we heard everywhere in public places that weekend, we talked about what had happened. We decided to get off the bus at my house and watch the news on TV. Our ability to grasp the significance of a news event absent pictures of it was atrophied by a short but intense lifetime of television-watching.

Sharing thoughts and opinions that probably exceeded the grasp of most high school freshmen and thirteen years of life experience, we discussed the effect President Kennedy's assassination would have on life in America after that Friday.

Adams said we'd probably have to work much harder at enjoying it.

He was right.

We did.

We still do.

CHAPTER ONE

I would finally appear at Jonathan Adams's front door almost nine months after he had returned from Iraq. I stayed four days. Lesions made by Iraq's jagged edges seemed mostly mended by then. But one deep gash remained. It had festered since he'd been home.

"Time heals all wounds" is as true and instructive a phrase as any four words strung together in the English language. But a part of me believes I could have done something to help accelerate my friend's healing process. Maybe things would have turned out differently if I'd been there when Adams made his first attempts to wash Iraq from his dirty clothes and shake her from his dusty shoes.

*

We were almost past Adams's mailbox when my driver noticed the address written boldly in black enamel paint on its silver sides. His cab barely missed the mailbox when he made a last-second sharp right into Adams's driveway.

Adams's impressive two-story black-shuttered gray house loomed in front of us. It grew larger as the taxi meandered up its neat, narrow driveway, lined on both sides by maple trees more robust than saplings, but not yet mature.

This was actually the second home built on its foundation. The first one was only two years old when a tornado blew it away in 1975, along with the family of four who lived in it. The people who bought the property three years later designed and built the house that stands there now. Twelve years after they moved in, they were killed in an automobile accident while vacationing in Canada. The stockbroker from Minneapolis who bought it a year later broke his neck when he fell off a ladder; he'd been trying to a remove a bird's nest from the chimney cap. It had been Adams's house for almost six years when I visited him in late September. Until then, he'd been unaffected by the tragedy that seeped into the lives of everybody who had ever lived on his hill.

To be sure, the house and the property surrounding it were beautiful. But it was much too big a place for one person. Its size and its history would have been reasons enough to keep me house-hunting. But Jonathan Adams loved dancing on the rims of volcanoes. The house, its history, and the land all around it grabbed him when he stepped inside its reach, and never let him go. The place was tightly woven into his fabric.

My folded arms found their way to the top of the taxi's bench seat in front of me. I rested my chin and stared through the windshield at his colonnaded porch. The absence of a vehicle parked along the driveway told me I had beaten Jim Breech there.

My visit was overdue. Since that middle-of-the-night phone call almost a year earlier, and the shooting in Samarra six weeks later, our personal and professional obligations had prevented us from cobbling a few days to share together. As it turned out, the four days I would spend with my friend were mostly scheduled, but in a comfortable way that kept us from having to find things to do.

"Is this where Jonathan Adams lives?" my Somali driver asked. His accent was marked with traces of

British English.

"Do you know him?" I asked, surprised. It has always been difficult for me to absorb the fact that my best friend is moderately famous. He never acted like I supposed a famous person should act; he was too familiar to be any kind of a celebrity.

"Oh yes, sir, I know of him. Jonathan Adams is a good man. He has been very helpful to my community—to the Somalis who live here."

As if he had been standing picket duty at a hiding place in the shrubbery, Adams pounced on the taxi the moment it stopped in front of his house. He bear-hugged me before I was hardly out of the car. The spontaneous gesture was an awkward, unusual show of emotion for both of us. Realizing that, Adams pushed us a handshake's length apart.

"It's great to see you, Tom," he gushed. He was grayer and thinner than I remembered from our last visit in New York.

He led me behind the taxi, where the driver was already pulling my bag from the trunk. Adams shook hands with the man, introduced himself, and asked him his name, where he lived, how long he had been in Minnesota, and how he and his family were adjusting to life in the United States.

I stood beside the cab and watched them talk, lost for a few seconds in random thought.

Adams was a man who aged well. He was in reasonably good shape and had managed to keep most of his hair. When we were kids, he would suck his cheeks into his mouth, making the sides of his face indent. When I asked him why he did this, he said that it would mold his face and give it more character as he grew into it. He compared it to lifting weights. He told me that every time his mother saw a Gregory Peck movie on television, she would say how handsome he was. Adams decided that the lines in Peck's face and the hollow spots beneath his cheekbones gave him his distinctive and quietly confident look. Adams liked the look. He decided he should emulate it after Peck got an Academy Award for his role as Atticus Finch in *To Kill a Mockingbird*.

Much to the consternation of a hundred housewives in our hometown, Adams beat all of them to the bookmobile the summer of 1962 and checked out the traveling library's only copy of Harper Lee's novel. He managed to keep it half of June and all of July. He read it twice during those six weeks. The film was made shortly after the book was published. The closest movie theater was ten miles away. Our parents seemed uncomfortable when we mentioned anything about the book and talked about wanting to see the movie. Most adults in Maplewood, a third-ring, white, middle-class suburb of Cleveland, were bothered by the civil rights movement, race relations, and what was happening "down South." They wondered why "the coloreds" felt a need to stir everything up, instead of being "just a little more patient." When the movie came to the Bristol Theater our parents were too busy to drive us to see it.

Against my objections, Adams insisted on paying my cab fare.

"I should have picked you up at the airport. But I wasn't sure when Breech would get here, and your plane could have been late."

No explanation was required, but as always, Adams felt compelled to offer one. He had forgotten the fact that taking a cab from the airport had been my suggestion.

I'd offered it when he called me the Sunday before and told me that Jim Breech, a seminal part of our Wonder Bread years growing up in Maplewood, had called Adams out of the blue and suggested he could "stop by for a beer" sometime that Thursday on his way home to Ohio after a two-week fishing trip in Manitoba. Neither of us had seen or talked to Jim Breech in almost forty years. Adams insisted that I extend my planned visit, moving it up by two days to be on hand for the occasion. I eagerly complied. Seeing Breech again would be like having a second chance to get a look at Halley's Comet—a once-in-a-lifetime experience offered to those of us alive when it was scheduled to swing by.

Adams and I saw Halley's Comet at an observatory in California in 1986. We hoped that Jim Breech's reappearance wouldn't be as disappointing.

As the taxi headed back down his driveway, Adams picked up my bag, put his arm around my shoulders, and steered us up the walkway and through his bright-red front door. Ten minutes later, we were sitting on the long redwood deck attached to the back of his house, waiting for Breech and drinking cold beer from a chilled case of Rolling Rock that Adams had bought specially for Breech's visit.

*

Over the years, Adams and I learned how to bridge the wide gaps between the times we were in each other's company. We ignored them. If something happened during the interim that we felt was important, the news worked its way into the flowing conversation. An hour after Adams and I had toasted my presence on his back deck, ours was already in the midst of a lull. The quiet was more the symptom of a comfortable familiarity than any indication of a burned-out friendship.

Adams showed no fallout from his trauma in Iraq, though he seemed to be making a discernible effort to avoid the subject. I came to Minnesota determined to induce a detailed account of what happened to him in Iraq, so I could pull him back to where he was before he left. My first attempt occurred when we were standing in his kitchen, uncapping our first bottles of beer. Adams asked about my sister. I made my move. I told him that her youngest son returned home last year from an eight-month tour of duty near Tikrit.

Adams nibbled, but chose not to take the bait. "He must have been based at Camp Speicher. The place is a hell hole: a patch of dusty desert, roofless cement-block buildings, a few scrubby trees, some brown grass, and lots of buckled blacktop."

Then I heard the story for the hundredth time about how he had always regretted not having made a run at Gina while the three of us were in high school.

"Your sister has the most beautiful brown eyes I've ever seen. They're unforgettable. They're truly something to behold."

As far as I know he hadn't seen my sister and her

brown eyes since my wedding in Connecticut a very long time ago. He handed me my beer and I followed him onto his back deck through the screen door he slid open.

Six billion people walked the earth that Thursday afternoon, and not one of them had been involved in as much of Adams's life as I had. Yet there was almost always a sliver of space between us. That was how he was. He allowed me glances at the intimate details of his life, but he shared very few of the feelings that surely accompanied them.

To a casual observer Adams seemed contemplative and sensitive. Sometimes he was inspiring. But I've never known anyone so ill at ease with his private side. He blossomed when circumstances thrust him into highly charged situations. But he needed more space and time than the rest of us to work through personal problems, most of which were self-inflicted. He was as incapable of managing his own life as he was abundantly blessed in his ability to take care of the rest of us. A pilgrim in the Land of Opportunity, Adams perpetually sought more, to fill a gnawing sense of emptiness he had no business feeling.

Alongside the fragility that almost no one ever saw, Adams was assembled with all the best attributes of our generation: curiosity, idealism, tenacity; elements that had gradually been beaten out of the rest of us by the demands and compromises of life that Adams had somehow managed to avoid—at least until Iraq.

As we talked on his back deck I looked for signs that he was pushing and pulling and shaping himself into what he used to be.

"I introduced a campaign finance bill last month; we had hearings on it last week," Adams said.

First indications were that my Byronic hero was back.

Adams paused and picked at the label on his beer bottle. "We got a fair amount of good press, but it's not likely to go anywhere. We have too few sponsors and there's a ton of money quietly working against us. The struggle's wearing me down and I've only been at it a few weeks."

The smile on my face dissipated. Faith and hope were eclipsed by cynicism and doubt in the space of a sentence. I was searching for what I wanted to see. I needed to be more clinical. Adams was like one of Claude Monet's paintings of sunflowers and Japanese bridges spanning lily ponds. His substance was most obvious and best appreciated if the person looking for it wasn't standing too close.

We talked about politics for a few more minutes. Then he broke off the conversation.

"I need to walk out front and get the mail. Relax and make yourself comfortable. I'll get us two fresh beers when I pass back through the kitchen." Adams rose from his chair, walked the length of his deck and disappeared around the corner of his house.

Suddenly I was alone. I looked around me for the perspective I sought.

Where a man comes from and where he lives speaks loudly about him. Where he was born and how he was raised shapes him; his house tells how he's processed that. Adams and his house showed great possibilities and a crate full of contradictions. Adams made no effort to hide the creature comforts he collected, available to Americans whose dreams have been largely realized— at least in economic terms. Signs of success were everywhere on display. A two-story floor-to-ceiling window separated most of the redwood deck from his sumptuous living room. Enclosed by a vaulted ceiling, the room was dominated by a massive stone fireplace. A covered hot tub occupied the north end of the deck; a large gas grill was pushed against the side of the house.

I was settled into one of four green canvas-backed chairs that neatly surrounded a classic, green beveled glass-topped, round patio table. Adams enjoyed the good life. He liked having his comfortable life style easily accessible but he indulged in it less frequently than most: The hot tub, gas grill, and fireplace looked too clean from where I sat.

The sliding door between his kitchen and deck screeched open. Adams passed through with two bottles of beer and an opened, official-looking envelope that he'd just picked up from his mailbox. He put them on the patio table and sat down across from me.

"Read this, Tom." It was a letter from the governor of Minnesota urging Adams to run for the position the governor himself was about to vacate. It pledged his support during the upcoming campaign.

"Wow," I said. "What are you going to do?"

"I've got a small folder full of letters like this and a couple dozen e-mails. I haven't responded to any of them yet. This should be the high-water mark of my career in politics, but I just can't muster the energy and focus I'll need to take the next step. To tell you the truth, Tom, I'm not sure I can do the job." His right hand shook slightly as he raised his beer bottle to his lips. "Besides the project I bungled in Iraq, it's been a long time since I've had to manage anything bigger than my senate staff."

Episodes of hypercritical self-assessment afflicted Jonathan Adams—like malaria does to people who have the disease. I've frequently witnessed his outbreaks. He should have been immune. That Thursday, the symptoms were bubbling inside him. They were beginning to ooze out through his pores. But just as he was about to break into an uncontrolled sweat, Adams did what he often does when he's caught face-to-face with himself: He changed the subject.

"Tom, what do you think about our reaction to this political/economic meltdown? How do you think people will handle doing more with less? Does our generation have the gumption to deal with hardship? Have we the ability anywhere inside us to defer gratification?"

I smiled. I knew what he was doing. I enabled him.

"It looks like our friends' grandchildren are going to be the first generation in American history whose quality of life won't be as good as what their parents enjoyed. You're the politician. How are you going to address selfishness, greed, and deal with no sense of community or pretense of civility?"

In spite of what he had said about running for governor, I was hoping he was still weighing his options. My words were meant to encourage him.

He raised his gaze from his beer bottle. "I'm on

the wrong side of public opinion these days, Tom. I'm damn lucky I live in the most liberal senate district in the state. I'm pro-choice, pro-gun control, and I support affirmative action programs." Adams paused and took a drink. "I was hammered in Hibbing last week when I spoke against a bill that would chop the legs out from under public-employee unions. I believe a school teacher's health care plan and retirement package ought to be models we emulate. Most of the people I'm acquainted with think it's a bloated fringe benefits package that should be shrunk to the size of a pea." He ran his finger around the rim of his green beer bottle. "I'm getting tired of going to town hall meetings and listening to people living on Social Security and Medicare demand that the government get out of their lives." Adams straightened himself in his chair. "That's a few of the reasons why I'm not the guy who ought to run for governor next year."

A shroud of silence temporarily covered the patio table.

"I wish I had the interest, energy, and the patience to grapple with the big issues of the day," he said wearily. "If only I were forty years old again." He peeled the green label off his sweating beer bottle. "I wish I didn't know now what I didn't know then."

"Bob Seger and the Silver Bullet Band: 'Against the Wind.'"

I did a poor job of singing the song's chorus. Adams laughed. Then we looked at each other too seriously, and he got up from his chair and walked over to the deck railing.

I'd lost him.

CHAPTER TWO

Standing with his back to me, his arms rigidly attached to the top railing of the deck, my friend was like a mechanical pen on one of those machines that measures earthquakes. I can't recall exactly how he resumed the conversation. But I remember the way his words crackled and scatted back and forth. Discussion pingponged between two disparate subjects: making choices and falling in love. Adams somehow managed to weave them together.

"What am I supposed to do with the rest of my life? Get married again and settle down? Move to California? Start a new career? Write a novel? Learn how to fly an airplane? I'm adrift and there's no shoreline in sight, Tom."

The sentences that spilled out of him filled blank pages in the first chapter of a familiar story. We'd had this talk before. But this time the narrative was more intense and substantial.

"I have no faith in things I used to believe were true and important. Iraq blew them up. I can't put Humpty Dumpty back together again."

Adams turned toward me, weakly smiled, and took a seat on the deck railing, one leg touching the deck, the other dangling in the air.

His journey back to normalcy had barely been abetted by Minnesota's safe harbor and sea of friendly faces. His sails were deployed, but everything was dead calm—not the relaxing kind of calm, but the stagnant kind.

"As usual, I've put myself at a place where the road branches off in different directions. I've been standing there ever since I got home. I'm afraid I might be stuck. I desperately need to fall in love, Tom, with somebody or something. What do I do?"

What he'd exclaimed seemed at first disconnected. During the brief quiet that followed, I thought about what he had said. It began to make sense.

Adams didn't wait for me to offer the advice he asked for. He shrugged his shoulders and continued: "The best thing that's happened to me lately is that I've been able to compartmentalize things." He told me that his gut-wrenching experiences in Iraq had been shoved into an untidy drawer. The drawer was finally closed and would be paid no attention for a while, he said. "I'll crack it open for you to peek inside, but I'm going to shut it closed after you get your look"

I moved to the edge of my chair and listened to him talk.

Three wonderful people in their full flower of life had been yanked from the earth on account of him, he reminded me. My mildly offered challenge to his indictment was chased away by the brush of his hand.

"The day after Hind, Farah, and Nur were killed, I ran straight into the fog of war, and stayed lost there for a while, on purpose. I got tangled up in things that were illegal, vengeful, and savage. I witnessed the torture of two of the men who were involved in the attack. After they finally confessed, we turned them over to Iraqi authorities. They never made it to the police station. They vanished. I knew they would. I paid ten thousand dollars to make it happen."

Adams moved off the railing, turned around, and faced his backyard. "I thought I could turn those feelings off when I stepped back in the world. It doesn't work that way."

That was all he said before he closed the drawer. He changed the topic so fast that I briefly worried about his sanity.

"God, I wish I could be in love. I need the distraction. I need the excitement love gives everything going on around it. The best way for me to recapture a passion for living is to throw myself into what I'm so god-awfully bad at."

I watched Adams closely. Like someone trying to teach himself how to swim by jumping into water over his head, he was flailing in a lake of proof that we can't control when we fall in love, nor do we have the ability to choose with whom it happens.

He stared blankly in the direction of a faraway stand of trees, a fallow field away. "The big, bad wolf is here and I'm the pig who built his house with straw."

With the exaggerated effort of a man over fifty, I left my chair and stiffly walked over to Adams. He was upright and rigid, his arms folded across his chest. He didn't acknowledge my presence with even a casual glance. My short trip over his redwood deck was made to remind him I was somewhere in the picture, available if he wanted to share more.

"I'm here to see if you're still breathing."

My clumsy attempt at humor blew by him, as snow flies past a gnarled fencepost in the middle of a January blizzard.

I turned my attention to where he stared. Our eyes saw the same panorama of an expansive restored prairie, bordered by a thin line of trees, gradually descending to a thick stand of maples and birch that hid a river at the slope's end, just out of sight. Adams's field of tall golden grass waved like a flag in the gentle breeze.

Before I could lose myself in the landscape, our silence was washed away in a cloudburst of Adams's thoughts.

"'A man without a cause is nothing. He has nothing to look forward to. He has nothing to work toward.' I wrote that down in a diary I kept when we were in high school. I have no idea who said it. I claimed it as my own a long time ago."

Adams turned and finally looked at me. "Have you ever worked hard to get somewhere you've always wanted to be, actually been in sight of it, and let it slip away? Have you ever been given something you've always wanted—had it simply fall in your lap? Have you ever lost what you've earned or been given because you did something stupid, or because you just plain didn't accept, understand, or appreciate the significance of it?"

He leaned back against the deck railing. He stretched, raised his arms toward heaven, and clasped his hands together behind his head. "Maybe I'm where I am because of the decisions I didn't make, rather than the decisions I made—because of what I failed to do, rather than what I did."

He turned away from me and faced west. With bowed head and lowered eyes, he cast his tribulation out over a freshly mowed lawn that separated his deck from his field of prairie grass, as if he were Saint Peter fishing with Jesus, throwing his net into the Sea of Galilee.

"How have I come to this point, alone and with nothing to show for it?" he mumbled.

The warm front that Adams took great care to show the world had collided with his concealed cold front to form a billowing cloud of gloom.

"I know why, I just don't know how."

He reached into his hip pocket, pulled out his wallet, and extracted a photo printed on a worn folded piece of white copy paper. He handed it to me. It was the picture that Hind had downloaded from her camera and e-mailed to him right before she was killed. I looked at it for a long time. I couldn't think of anything to say.

I glanced through the walls of Adams's house, hoping Jim Breech was turning into the driveway. I needed him to help me pull Adams out of the imperfect present and push all three of us back into our Arcadian past. I passed the picture back to him. He carefully refolded it.

Adams put his wallet back in his jeans pocket and brushed past where I stood, as if no one were there. He marched the length of his deck. I followed him halfway, taking a seat on the railing.

"The reason I'm alone and where I am is because I've managed to chase away every woman who's ever loved me."

His theory didn't surprise me. Since we were twelve years old, his recurrent self-critiques were inevitable, predictable, and almost always traceable to women. He enjoyed spending time with women and he needed to be around them. The things they said and did expressed the acceptance, admiration, and encouragement he craved.

Serenity and consistency signaled his involvement in a steady and exclusive relationship. More likely were a string of exuberant connections with younger women—all of them beautiful and creative, every one of them initiators of their brief entanglements, which burned bright like flares shot out over a battlefield. These affairs drained Adams. He claimed that exhaustion was a fair price for a few consecutive weeks of not having to act his age. That Thursday he was dormant and lethargic—someplace in between—sleeping alone.

"I need to be in love again. I need another chance at it," Adams concluded. "I know how to fall in love, but I don't know how to stay in love. Can I learn how to give all of me up? I've never done that. I don't know if I can pull it off at this stage in my life. I live how I drive, Tom. I've been cruising in the passing lane, ten miles an hour over the speed limit, for as long as I can remember. It's fast enough to get me where I'm going before almost everyone else—fast enough to get noticed but not a speed that demands attention or threatens anybody's safety—at least until Iraq."

Adams looked down at the deck and rubbed his forehead. "My rearview mirror is suddenly filled with the silver grill of a Mack truck hauling a heavy load of reality and squandered time."

I looked at him and frowned. Adams was consumed by the blast of the truck's bellowing horn. But he was incapable of changing lanes.

*

I was sitting on the rail, facing the wall of glass that looked into his living room, when my eyes were diverted to a gaping wound in a neat row of gray cedar shingles above the frame of the doorway that separated the deck from his kitchen. A white chalk circle and yellow police tape marked the place where a shingle had split. A hole the size of a golf ball had been dug into the exposed wooden beam. I pushed away from the railing. Adams was talking again but I wasn't listening. I walked to the place and reached up. I could barely touch the spot. It was large enough and deep enough for me to be able to probe it with two fingers.

From the far end of his deck, Adams stopped and stared. He was anticipating my question and appeared to be forming a careful answer.

This was the fourth time I had been to Adams's house since he had moved into it. His house perpetually looked like it was about to be photographed for *Architectural Digest*. The only room that looked lived in was a converted downstairs bedroom that he used as an office. A broken cedar shingle with a chalk-marked hole was easily noticed. I am a trained observer, after all. How could I have missed it?

"That's a bullet hole," he said. "The police dug the bullet out of the beam behind the shingle and bagged it for evidence. They think someone might have taken a shot at me last Monday evening."

My jaw dropped. I was more stunned by the casual manner in which Adams offered his explanation than I was by its content.

He continued, matter-of-factly: "The police found a rifle with a scope out in the field, just beyond where the lawn ends and the prairie starts." He pointed in the general direction. As if on cue, a police car drove slowly through the prairie grass, along a hidden rutted tractor path Adams allowed a neighboring farmer to use to access his corn and bean fields. The path was halfway between where we stood and the far, forested west end of his property that hid the river that marked its boundary.

"The police are more concerned about this than I am. They've been watching things pretty carefully since Monday night. I feel like I'm living in a fishbowl. That's the third time I've seen a police car down there."

Adams stopped, waiting for a response so he could temper the tenor of his story to it. I offered none.

"I think it was an accident, and I told the police that. It was probably a kid wandering around in the field out there, looking for a rabbit or a turkey to shoot at. Anyway, it was quite an experience. I heard the shot and ducked, an instant after the bullet whistled past my head. It literally whistled past my head. I think I actually felt the bullet brush by my face. Right after I ducked, I looked out over the railing, out at the field—the place where I figured the shot had come from. I saw someone running through the tall grass, toward the woods and the river. If the person with the rifle were really trying to shoot me, he would have stayed where he was and taken another shot. Don't you think so? It had to have been a stray shot from a mischievous kid doing something he shouldn't have been doing, somewhere he shouldn't be doing it. You're not too old to have forgotten when we used to get ourselves into those kinds of predicaments, are you, Tom?"

Adams's eyes opened wider, his expression fatherly.

"It had to be something like that. I haven't been involved with anybody's girlfriend, daughter, or wife lately. And when is the last time you heard of a part-time state legislator being assassinated? We're not that high on the power ladder."

Adams laughed out loud. I smiled, but only slightly. Why would a panicked kid be hunting rabbits with a rifle that had a sniper's scope on it?

During the telephone conversation we had after Adams returned home from Iraq, he mentioned he had spent his last two months in Iraq pursuing the people who killed his staff, generating leads for the police investigation. He had paid Iraqis who lived and worked in his compound for any information they had about who might have organized the killings. He passed what he learned on to the remnants of U.S. Army intelligence that lingered in Iraq after most of our troops had gone home. Earlier in our conversation on his deck, he'd confessed to me his active involvement in the torture killings.

His effectiveness as a vigilante counterterrorism agent earned him a middle-of-the-night passage out of the country through a Kurdish/Turkish checkpoint, instead of a more routine, predictable, and unprotected road trip to the army base in Mosul, a helicopter ride to Baghdad, and a flight to Jordan. In spite of the secrecy that surrounded his departure, his three-car convoy was ambushed halfway between Mosul and Dahuk. His security people drove through it. Adams had touched nerves in the insurgency reforming in Iraq. He had helped roll up a few of its leaders. Al Qaeda was upset about it.

Back in the United States, Adams wrote a controversial article for the *Atlantic Monthly*. Expanding the main points he'd made in a *New York Times* op-ed, Adams' article was a stinging critique of Muslim fundamentalists; it effectively argued that their strict interpretation of the Koran would doom their brand of Islam. The leaders of the movement and a dwindling band of followers were condemned to irrelevance in ten years' time, he wrote—especially after oil reserves depleted and the price of a barrel of oil approached two hundred dollars. That circumstance, Adams maintained, would finally cause the rest of us to get more creative and become less dependent on oil as our main source of energy. When that happened, the Middle East would become more like sub-Saharan Africa, and we'd ignore it accordingly.

Besides stirring up a robust debate inside the Muslim community about al Qaeda's bankrupt version of Islam, the article resulted in a fatwa being issued by a prominent radical cleric in Pakistan. The fatwa decreed that any Muslim who managed to kill or maim Jonathan Adams would earn the reward of a rich and enjoyable afterlife if he or she were killed during any kind of a credible attempt.

I'd feared for my friend's safety when he first told me what he had done during his last two months in Iraq. Those worries grew as I closely followed the swell of reaction to his *Atlantic Monthly* and *New York Times* articles. But my fears mostly evaporated as a few months' worth of cable TV news cycles came and went. Monday evening's shooting revived my concerns and intensified them exponentially. I was sure I knew the reason for what had happened.

"Winston Churchill said that there are few things in life more exhilarating than being shot at and missed," Adams said. He laughed softly, the understated laugh of a soldier talking around the outside edges of his experience in combat.

"The incident made me think less about what happened to my friends in Iraq. That day's been too much on my mind. So maybe the shooting had a positive effect." He laughed again. "Anyway, Jim Brandt, the farmer next door, happened to be walking along his north fence line when all this happened. He saw the rifle flash and heard the shot. He called the police. Not the way I would have handled things."

Adams walked to his patio table and sat down. I did the same.

"Monday must have been a slow night for the sheriff's office and the state highway patrol. Six police officers spent an awful lot of time here. A couple of FBI agents from the office in Minneapolis got involved on Tuesday. Fortunately, none of the neighbors seemed to be out and about. I made Brandt take a vow of silence about all this. There's no need having people around here thinking I'm the target of some kind of a mob hit, or worrying their family might get caught in the crossfire. You know how rumors spread."

Adams looked out beyond the deck. His eyes followed the path the bullet had taken from his field to his house. When he saw me watching him, he threw me the most calming smile he could muster. The look on his face said: If I can put the matter behind me, you should, too.

But in spite of his assurances, I found myself glancing nervously across the field as the day lengthened. The police car had crossed the prairie's width, turned around in an apple orchard, and was backtracking toward the county road.

CHAPTER THREE

I needed something more than Adams's explanation to sooth my worry. A welcome distraction came with Jim Breech's loud knock on the front door. What was left of my consternation and Adams's melancholy we shed behind as we quickly walked through his house. Breech stood ready, fist raised, to knock on the door again as Adams pulled it open. I was four steps behind him.

A full head taller than us, Jim Breech was fuller in the face and wider in the waist than I remembered him to be in high school. More gray than blond, the front part of his hair was waxed a half inch straight up from the top of his head—the same way it was the last time

I had seen him in the early 1970s. But his hairline had been fighting a losing battle since then. In fact, there wasn't really much hair left on his head behind what remained of his rooster comb. Breech's short hair and the gray long-sleeved sweatshirt he was wearing that had *ARMY* stenciled boldly across it in black letters made him look like a thirty-year-veteran sergeant major who was ready to make life hell for a platoon of recruits.

Breech thrust his long arm across the threshold at Adams, inviting a handshake that Adams instantly provided. Breech's broad smile pulled me closer to the doorway.

"J.J., you haven't changed a bit," he bellowed. Glancing over Adams's shoulder, he said, "Tom Walker, what the hell are you doing here?"

Breech had christened Adams "J.J." shortly after they met on the first day of fourth grade. His unchallenged status as our greatest local athlete made the nickname stick. It was seldom applied to Adams by anyone besides Breech, and the tradition died soon after high school graduation—as quickly as Breech dropped out of our lives.

Still standing in the doorway, Breech began his visit with an apology.

"Like I told you on the phone, J.J., in order to get permission from Margie to spend a week up in Canada fishing with my suppliers, and stop in and see you on my way back, I had to promise her, my daughter, and my two grandkids that I'd meet them in Wisconsin Dells Thursday night on the way home. Well, it's Thursday, and I figure it's a five-hour drive down to the Dells from here. So I've got to leave in a couple of hours. Sorry I can't stay longer."

"Let's see how much we can pack into those two hours," Adams offered as he ushered big Jim Breech into his house.

"So where does somebody go to get a beer here?" Breech asked as he ambled through the foyer. Adams and I stepped out of his way as he strode past us and headed down the hallway, looking for a refrigerator. His familiar manner spanned thirty years in ten seconds. Adams and I knew nothing about three people Breech had just mentioned: a daughter and two grandchildren. That confirmed the two-generation gap in time jammed between us.

In twenty minutes' time, Adams had given Breech the obligatory tour of his house and thirty years were backfilled with rough summaries of our separate lives since high school. We let Breech do most of the work.

His long pauses after our short answers suggested he was weighing the heft of our responses against what his would be when his turn came to account for the time. The expression on Breech's face and his having asked neither of us for elaboration about anything we said told me that we were evidence that his horse, so quickly and splendidly out of the starting gate, was trailing as we were passing the three-quarters pole and approaching the finish line. I figured self-assessment had been as heavy on his mind as it had been on Adams's. It surely had something to do with the considerable effort Breech must have made to find Adams, lost from Maplewood for most of his lifetime. Adams sensed the same thing; a quick glance my way told me so.

Jim Breech had married Margie Rice the month before they began their senior year at Kent State University. Margie was his high school sweetheart and the girl our graduating class voted most popular. Breech received a scholarship to play basketball and baseball at the University of Pennsylvania. By the end of his fifth week on campus, he was feeling lonely and unappreciated, far away in Philadelphia. A disappointing sophomore season playing basketball at Penn finally drove him back to Maplewood, with the intention of finishing college close to home. He happily returned to Margie's arms.

Everything that had happened to Breech after that was news to us that Thursday afternoon.

By 1990, Jim and Margie had married each other twice and divorced each other once. Their staccato relationship produced two children: a daughter, Angie, and a son, James. James was killed in Kuwait in 1991, a KIA in the almost casualty-free first Gulf War. One of Saddam's scud missiles hit his mess hall while he was eating breakfast. Jim's daughter, Angie, and his twelve-year-old twin granddaughters lived in Chicago and were waiting for him with Margie in Wisconsin Dells. Breech made no mention of a son-in-law.

"And I'm still working at the lumberyard in Maplewood," he announced. Jim Breech was the owner of the lumberyard now. More significantly, he was CEO of the thriving big-box home improvement center that had grown up next to it.

When we lived in Maplewood, a summer job working for Larry Hansen at his sprawling south-side lumberyard was prestigious and paid well. Mr. Hansen had been the school board president for as long as anybody could remember. There was always a place on his payroll during the summer for the school's best varsity athletes. The fathers of kids who were imported from West Virginia, western Pennsylvania, and southern Ohio to play on the high school football team could count on finding jobs there, too. Breech started working for Hansen when he was sixteen. The only time Adams and I were permitted to wander inside the ten-foot-high chain-link fence that surrounded Hansen's business was when we helped my father load two-by-fours and paneling onto a rented trailer one springtime Saturday morning—building materials to be used in a never-ending effort to convert our two-car garage into a family room. For my father, it was a weekend do-it-yourself project that turned into a six-year hobby.

Larry Hansen eagerly offered Jim Breech a job in his sales department when he graduated with a bachelor's degree in business administration from Kent State. In four years' time, Breech headed the sales department; in four more, he was Hansen's business manager, his second-in-command. When Hansen retired, Breech bought half the business. He was elected to fill an open seat on the school board when one of its senior members moved up to succeed Hansen as school board president. That was twelve years ago.

Empty Rolling Rock bottles were beginning to clutter the glass top of the patio table. We took turns making trips to the kitchen refrigerator to fetch full, cold ones. By the time it was my turn, Breech had told us as much of his life story as he wanted to. He was slumped in his chair, looking languidly at the other end of the deck.

Twenty years in the publishing business had taught me how to stimulate a lagging conversation, how to break down the kinds of walls years of disparate life experience builds between authors, publishers, literary agents, and readers. I jumped headfirst into the void. "Did either of us ever get a hit off you in Little League, Jim?" I asked. "I don't think I ever did."

Adams sensed what I was trying to do. "Come on, Tom. Don't you remember? I hit a sixth inning broken-bat single off him once. Cost him a no-hitter, I recall," he said with a satisfied smile. "And our friend Jim Breech shouldn't let the fact that you never got a hit off him during your entire career in organized baseball go to his head. Hell, Tom—everybody who ever pitched to you no-hit you."

It was a nearly true statement, and drew a hardy laugh from Breech. I didn't mind.

"I still have stitch marks on my butt cheek where Jim plunked me with the first curveball I ever thought I saw," Adams announced. He stood up from his chair, threatening to show us.

Breech was already more than six feet tall when we were twelve years old. When he started a pitch just forty-six feet away from you—the length a pitcher stood from the batter in Little League—his stride seemed to carry him halfway to home plate before the ball left his hand. Unless we mortals had already started to swing the bat before Breech released the ball, and had somehow guessed correctly where it would be when it crossed home plate a fraction of a second later, there was little chance the bat we fearfully gripped too tightly would ever touch a baseball he threw.

Breech liked listening to us talk about him as if he weren't there. He enjoyed his Maplewood fame in a pleasant, modest way. We had successfully recharged his battery. He straightened himself in his chair, moving closer to its edge as he leaned over the table and thrust his large hand into what was left of a wooden salad bowl filled with Chex Mix.

"Tom, remember when J.J. got into his first varsity basketball game against Western Reserve our junior year? Remember when he blocked that layup after they got a pass behind him on that full-court zone press we used to run all the time?"

Merely referencing the incident made me recall that night in all of its detail. A smile that quickly grew big enough to fill half of Adams's face said that he remembered, too.

Prompted by Breech, Adams finished the story. "The gym was full of people—standing room only, as it always was for those games. Remember how loud the place got? But I could still hear Coach Temple's voice cut through all the noise: 'Adams, what the hell are you doing!' We were probably twenty points ahead with only a minute to play, but I knew I'd pay for it at practice on Monday if I screwed up at the end of the fourth quarter that Saturday night."

Breech interrupted: "I swear, the kid from Western Reserve was standing under the basket with the ball in his hands when J.J recovered at the half-court line, after overplaying a pass he anticipated that never happened. No doubt extremely motivated by our beloved coach's suggestion that he correct his error, J.J. was suddenly on the poor kid, flying three feet over him. He pinned the kid's shot against the backboard!"

"I moved faster and jumped higher than I ever have," Adams proudly added.

"And the crowd went wild!" I shouted, with appropriate inflection. The three of us toasted an event that we had long forgotten about with a clink of our half-empty beer bottles after we rose from our chairs, meeting somewhere over an empty wooden salad bowl in the middle of a patio table.

Revived, Breech was the raconteur for our second hour together. The discussion Breech led was a warehouse full of recollections long ago left in the dust of Adams's haste to get some place beyond Maplewood. I watched Adams as he listened; he was mesmerized by Breech. I had seen that expression on his face before. When the three of us were growing up in Maplewood, Adams aspired to be just like Jim Breech—admired and respected, cool under fire, unfazed by the simulated crises that Maplewood cast our way. Breech liked Adams, and everyone knew it. I benefited because I was Adams's best friend. Being the best friend of one of Jim Breech's best friends markedly boosted my social standing in high school. Such was the potency of Breech's charisma in the thin air that flowed through the corridors of Maplewood High. Whatever possible benefit a Jim Breech endorsement might have provided me had long since disappeared. But sensing more than half a lifetime later that people back then may have thought I sported that advantage caused me to think more favorably about the time I spent in Maplewood; it seemed like a friendlier place.

As we galloped toward the end of Breech's visit, Adams sought to find out more about the contemporary Jim Breech. When Adams tried to draw him into a conversation about the issues his school board was facing, Breech turned a terse response into an announcement that one of our classmates, Richard Miller, had reappeared in Maplewood two years ago to audit a Department of Education grant the school district had received. A story about Richard Miller taking Adams's sister, Sharon, to our senior prom followed. With expansive gestures and well-placed adjectives and adverbs Breech reminded us how unglued Adams became when he found out that his little sister, a sophomore, would be part of his senior year's biggest social event. Adams gave up probing Breech and we laughed until our sides hurt.

Jim Breech looked at his watch. Our last hour was winding down. He apologized again for having had to make the visit so short, considering the long interlude since he had last seen us. He bridged the expanse of time with his last story.

"A kid named Marcus Jackson broke my Maplewood High single-season and career scoring records last March. Those records had stood for more than forty years. The athletic director and the basketball coach invited me to attend the home game where everybody expected it would happen." Breech buried his chin into the neckline of his sweatshirt. "I didn't want to go, but Margie made me. I'm on the school board, I'm a prominent figure in the community, so I could hardly turn the invitation down, she said. She told me that being there would be the gracious thing to do; 'magnanimous' was the word she used. She said it would enhance my image and benefit our business."

An uncomfortable silence filled the deck.

Breech continued: "Shaking the kid's hand, smiling during the ceremony at half court after the game, and telling a sixteen-year-old reporter for the school newspaper and Hal Barker from the *Maplewood Post* that I always expected my records would be broken were the most difficult things I've had to do in a very long time—maybe since we buried Jimmy. I've never admitted that to anyone before now."

Breech looked up at us and painfully smiled. His confession was followed by more intense quiet.

"Today's game is different than the game we played, J.J. You can't compare what this Jackson kid accomplished to what we did. They play at least twenty games a season now, instead of eighteen. You get three points for baskets you make that are eighteen feet from the hoop instead of just two. My god, this kid played at least ten more games than me during his varsity career."

Breech stopped. He seemed embarrassed by his outburst. Adams and I glanced nervously at each other.

Breech gathered himself together, un-shrugged his shoulders and pulled himself up straighter in his chair. "Got to go, guys. Margie and the girls will get nervous if I'm not at the Dells by eleven o'clock." He grimaced as he stood. "Bad knees—all I've got to show for it now."

The three of us stood silently around the patio table for too long before anyone moved.

"Let's go this way," Adams finally said.

Breech and I followed Adams across his deck.

When we passed the open sliding door to the kitchen, Breech glanced up at the bullet hole above the door. Adams turned around to see what had become of us. Watching Breech stop and stare at the wound in his wall, Adams shot me a look that clearly said we weren't going to talk about it unless Breech specifically asked what happened.

He didn't.

Adams rounded us up and led us down the deck's steps, across his lawn, and around his house to the driveway.

We shook hands with Breech and he climbed into his Jeep Cherokee. He started the engine and rolled down his window.

"Your shingle over the patio door is a Hardiplank 4306. We got six pallets full of them delivered to the store right before I left for Canada. If you've already ordered replacements, cancel the order. When I'm back at work on Monday, I'll ship a box up to you. That's enough to cover eight board feet."

Adams quickly accepted his offer and thanked him for it. Breech was happy. His smile told us that being able to help Adams made him feel important and useful, maybe even valued.

We shook hands again through Breech's open window and repeated our good-byes. As his Jeep started down the driveway, Adams and I smiled at each other. Breech's visit would no doubt inspire lots of thoughtful discussion during the rest of my visit.

Twenty yards away the Jeep suddenly stopped. Breech backed the car up to where we were still standing and pushed his head out of the window. "If I can get some of the guys from the basketball team together for a weekend in Florida this winter, would you two come down and play some golf?"

We said we would, that it sounded like a great idea. Jim Breech smiled again. As he started back down the driveway, he waved, grinning at us through his rearview mirror. Then he turned onto the road in front of Adams's house and disappeared from our lives again.

CHAPTER FOUR

With Breech barely out of the driveway, Adams asked, "What's worse, Tom: to be haunted for the rest of your life by something that happened to you when you were growing up, or to be stuck there?" I thought for a few steps and responded by reciting the lyrics of Bruce Springsteen's "Glory Days." By the time we got to the back deck we were doing a poor job singing it.

Adams cleared the patio table and disappeared into the kitchen. He put his wooden bowl in the dishwasher and our empty bottles in the open beer case on the floor next to his refrigerator. It took two trips for him to haul in the bottles. He insisted on doing the job himself.

Maggie once admonished me for putting wooden bowls in the dishwasher. Wooden bowls should be hand-washed, she said. I decided that wasn't worth mentioning as I watched Adams through the screen door. I was left on the deck to ponder his question about guilt and stunted growth. Thoughts about Jim Breech's visit pulsed through my brain like jets of gas in the brightly colored tubes of a blinking neon sign. I couldn't get Springsteen's music out of my head.

I decided that Jim Breech had probably begun to drift away from Adams and me as early as the tenth grade, when we started to develop different political philosophies. Just as importantly, we were in different homerooms for the first time and only shared half the classes that we used to.

Adams and I fancied the two of us to be on the short list of the best things Maplewood ever produced. Expectations were low for anything significant that was non-athletic to come from Maplewood. Distinction was a goal to which we were taught to aspire, but a goal we knew we never really needed to achieve in order to be judged successful. We learned that the broad, comfortable middle of the bell curve was the safest place to be.

That was the context in which Adams and I confronted the conflicted relationship almost everyone seems to have with the place where they grew up. But on Adams's deck that Thursday afternoon, Maplewood began to blossom into something worth a second look. Pleasant memories were popping into my head like perennials that sprout in a neglected garden after a warm springtime rain. Our town could never be described as a greenhouse for innovation. But maybe Maplewood was someplace in between–like an old flannel shirt— comfortable, never trendy, but never out of style.

I speculated about what might have become of me if I, like Breech, had never really left Maplewood. I parked those thoughts in a safe place; Adams would surely want to talk about all this.

I walked to the deck railing. Looking out over Adams's backyard, I envisioned Monday evening's shooting, wading deeper into the process of honing a theory as to why it happened.

Suddenly, my attention was hijacked by a familiar picture that had been hibernating for a very long time in another part of my brain. It was Jim Breech's fault that I was thinking about these kinds of things. I was staring out at the same landscape that I saw in the early afternoon. But I was looking at it through a different prism now. Like one of those pictures hidden within a picture, I recognized it. Now I could never view what spread out behind Adams's house without seeing it: The scene beyond his back deck was a portrait of the eighty acres of raw land on which our neighborhood in Maplewood was built.

It was Byron's Lane—before Byron's Lane.

*

Maplewood first found its way onto a map in the mid-nineteenth century. It was a water stop for steam engines at the junction of two rail lines. The main line was built along a canal right-of-way that bankrupted its owners before the ditch they paid to be dug was ever filled with water.

The train tracks in the old canal bed had been abandoned by the time our eyes first fell upon our strange but ordinary community. A hundred years later, with our sudden presence on its doorstep, Maplewood transformed itself. In the wink of an eye it grew from a sagging water tower surrounded by a stagnant village of white wood-framed houses into giant tracts of basement-less ranch-style homes on eight-thousand-square-foot lots.

Enough single-family homes were built in Maplewood from 1956 through 1960 to comfortably contain more than thirty thousand people. Instant neighborhoods spread out across the top of the wide terminal moraine that Maplewood straddled—the southern-most point that an Ice Age glacier had pushed a colossal pile of rocks there fourteen thousand years ago. Lake Erie, the big hole from which most of Maplewood's stones had come, was once visible from the town's highest point on a clear day. But those days became rare, then nonexistent, as the land between our ridge and the lake filled up with houses, streets, stores, and factories; streams and rivers turned brown.

Maplewood was a conflicted place. It provided us the opportunity to assimilate and grow what became the basis for the better angels of our nature. It provided a safe, nurturing environment. It offered the time and the space we needed to develop into useful worker bees. As we grew into adults, we echoed Maplewood's good and bad aspects. The bad things we did weren't really that bad—they were nearsighted and inconsiderate. We did them because we believed they would make good things happen. Our self-confidence was peppered with brashness. We learned to enjoy eating steak by smothering it with ketchup. We watched our parents dilute one part top-shelf vodka with four parts Minute Maid frozen orange juice. We seasoned our view of the world with half a teaspoon of racism. We were taught that selfishness could be construed as virtuous if applied in ways that made our families safe and secure.

I escaped Maplewood by marrying into a family that owned and managed a respected boutique publishing business in New York. I met Maggie and fell in love with her our sophomore year at Ohio State. My weekend with Adams coincidentally marked my twentieth year as the publishing company's president.

Adams affected his getaway by attending college in Chicago and converting a doctoral thesis about relationships between land use, economic development, and property taxation into a book that became and remains required reading for public administration students, city managers, urban planners, and thoughtful mayors.

Jonathan Adams tried harder than me to shed Maplewood. I appreciated our hometown for having introduced me to a great steak and good vodka. Adams couldn't shake the bad memories of a dinner at Kathy's father's country club in Bethesda, the first time she took him home to Washington, two years before they graduated from Northwestern and married. He asked the bartender to put ice cubes and a splash of water in his first glass of twenty-year-old single malt Scotch and reminded the waiter that he had forgotten to put a bottle of ketchup on their table.

When people asked Adams where he had grown up, he'd say Ohio. He never said Maplewood. But Byron's Lane always seemed to hold him tightly in its grasp, like the weedy vines a few feet from where I stood on his deck that strangled a neglected lilac bush that had overwhelmed what was left of a cord of firewood stacked next to the deck's steps.

Jim Breech, Jonathan Adams, and I were baby boomers, along with eighty percent of the population that lived in Maplewood when it first exploded onto the map—the big snake America has never been able to digest us as we've moved from its head to its tail. We were Maplewood's pride and joy and its unrivaled center of attention. We were children who were older than the neighborhoods that formed us. We were the first generation of Americans who were products of the American Dream, not participants in it. We didn't have to earn its fruits, they were bestowed upon us.

Our attitudes and demeanor reflected our circumstances and environment. Respect for the lessons of history, appreciation for the blessings that geography afforded us, family traditions and family ties—they all faded away as we floated through the public school system. Our drift produced a lifelong inability to put our lives into perspective. We faced no real challenges while growing up; we had no hardships to overcome, except artificial tests created by the games we played, our school's grading system, and our deep need to be a cherished member of a group. Our privileged, plain-vanilla lives afforded us no context for evaluating what we experienced. We grew into adults with tendencies to overreact to life's small problems, who failed to appreciate the significance of its large ones. We were so sure that our lives were different from anything our parents and grandparents had ever known that their stories had no relevance for us. We had no patience or inclination to sit and listen to them.

*

I first met Jonathan Adams at a place that looked just like his Minnesota backyard, when our fathers' identical red Ford station wagons, coming from different directions, pulled up and parked at the same time on the recently widened gravel shoulder of County Road 106. The location was soon to become the south end of Byron's Lane.

It was early April. Eight car doors opened and the

nine of us poured out, two husbands, two wives, and five kids, all eyes looking north. Adams and I would name the place El Capitan after we saw an Ansel Adams photograph in *Life* magazine of a larger, more impressive pile of rocks in California with the same name. We looked out over a scarred landscape, pockmarked by cement blocks uniformly arranged in thirty-by-seventy foot and thirty-by-eighty foot rectangles. They were anchored in mud, at intervals of forty feet. On most of the gray cement-block foundations rose pale yellow-brown skeletons of houses.

The wooden frames and rectangular foundations stretched out in four parallel rows, for almost as far as we could see. They were lined up equidistant on both sides of rutted navigation lanes that seemed to be flowing downhill. Byron's Lane was marked by two parallel rows of white wooden stakes, ten yards from each other, pounded into the soft ground by someone before someone else came along and poured a hundred truckloads of gravel between them.

Mr. Adams hopped up on the open tailgate of his Ford Ranch Wagon to get a better view. I remember him pointing to the distant tree line where the white stakes that marked Byron's Lane disappeared. The image reminded me of a painting reprinted in almost every American history textbook, in the chapter about Manifest Destiny: a frontier scout in buckskins, standing in the foreground, pointing westward, his charges in the background leading their ox-driven wagons in the direction he was pointing—a gap in the Allegheny Mountains. "Down there. That's where ours is," he announced.

My family and a few displaced blackbirds perched above us on hastily strung telephone wires couldn't help but overhear him. Adams's pregnant mother smiled at her husband's words, but had tears in her eyes that welled up and began to flow down pink cheeks that grew rosier the more they were watered. As his mother shed her happy tears, his two younger sisters emitted high-pitched squeals that both Adams and I learned to loathe the older we got and the more we heard them.

Our house would eventually rise from one of the cement-block foundations laid halfway between Adams's lot and where we stood. My parents, my sister, and I looked out in silence over the scene so boisterously framed by Adams's father. That was our style. We communicated telepathically in my family, by way of a sophisticated vocabulary of facial expressions. Our family peculiarity made me hypersensitive to nonverbal expression. I've lived my life quietly and carefully, like a white-tailed deer in an urban forest.

My first conversation with Jonathan Adams began ten minutes after we had first cast our eyes on Byron's Lane.

"I think this place used to be a prairie and home to a thousand buffalos a hundred years ago. What do you think?" he asked me.

"Maybe," I answered. "Look over there—corn stalks. I bet this was a big cornfield last year. Wouldn't it have been fun hiding in it, a hundred people looking for us, and no one could ever find us?"

My new best friend was sure the blackbirds, agitated, crackling and whistling overhead, could have told us what it all looked like last summer—but not in front of our families. That was the year Adams thought he could teach animals to communicate with him in long and short grunts, like the Morse code that he had just learned in Cub Scouts. Regardless, the birds' answers would have been drowned out by the cacophony of men putting hammer to nail, the racing diesel engines of cement trucks and bulldozers, and the cars driving past us on the gravel road. By Labor Day weekend and forever after, the noise of carpenters and earthmoving equipment had given way to the sounds of children, delivery trucks, and gasoline-powered lawnmowers.

Countless times during the next ten years, Adams and I ran, walked, or rode our bicycles the two blocks up Byron's Lane from my house to El Capitan, just off the S-curve on County Road 106, which had been renamed Cambridge Drive. Our favorite vantage point was sitting on a broad limb of an ancient, dying elm tree that we were sure was older than George Washington. The big tree had somehow grown on the knob of a round top that ascended from the other side of the road where our fathers' station wagons had parked. The protuberance was full of huge rocks, which probably saved it from being flattened and becoming a building site. It afforded an outstanding view of the neighborhood, particularly in the late autumn, winter, and early spring, when leaves on the other trees that grew from the rocks weren't hanging around to foul it.

The housing developer chose an English Romantic Period theme for his Maplewood subdivision. By the end of the first year of our neighborhood's existence, literary new street names had swept away all of Maplewood's more descriptive place names on our side of town. Gravel Pit Road was no more; Ridge Road disappeared from street signs; Cemetery Hill was gone forever. When it was finished, our instant neighborhood consisted of nine blocks: two north-south streets, bisected by two that ran east and west. We never counted how many houses made up the neighborhood, spread over a grid that resembled a giant tic-tac-toe board. But when Adams and I shared a *Cleveland Plain Dealer* route, we had 282 Sunday customers.

When I think of a lane, my mind drifts to the drive up to Scarlett O'Hara's antebellum mansion in *Gone with the Wind*, or a jeep trail under a canopy of oaks. No trees were ever planted to umbrella the exposed asphalt surface of Byron's Lane. The road was straight as an arrow, with no evidence anywhere along its sides of absolutely anything asymmetrical. Byron's Lane was hardly a lane at all.

*

I didn't notice that Adams had left his kitchen and returned to the deck. His silence and his posture told me that he had reverted to his reflective mood. I moved closer to the place where he stood. I wanted to share my epiphany with him.

His property slid down a long, gentle slope of grassland dotted by small clumps of brush. Besides our childhood neighborhood, the landscape was twin to the place at Gettysburg where Pickett's Charge had taken place during the Civil War. The tree line in the distance was where the Confederates assembled and began their march. Adams's deck was the stone wall at Cemetery Ridge that protected the Union soldiers. Gettysburg, Pennsylvania, was a long but manageable Sunday drive from Maplewood. Adams and I did it once during our senior year in high school and twice during the two summers we were home from college. Adams's grandfather was a soft touch when we needed a car for a road trip.

I excitedly told Adams what I saw hidden in the panorama of his property. Lumping Adams's backyard with two places we associated with lost causes—Byron's Lane and Pickett's Charge—produced a chuckle.

"You might be right," was all he said.

I noted the expression on his face. "You look like someone's just guessed the password for your ATM card."

"Yeah, right," he sarcastically replied. His response was too quick and too dismissive. He asked for no elaboration; he offered no further comment. He turned and passed by me, walking the length of his deck to fetch a paper napkin that had fallen off the patio table. On his way back to where I stood, he disappeared into his house through the sliding screen door.

Not knowing if Adams was planning to return,

I started to walk toward the door. But he reappeared three steps before I got there, filling the threshold with his broad-shouldered frame. Seconds later he was sitting across the table from me, pushing another bottle of Rolling Rock in my direction.

"Name an experience you had while we were growing up in Maplewood that affected the rest of your life," I said. "There must have been at least a few."

Adams looked up at me quizzically. His smile told me that he liked the question. I was surprised how quickly he responded. It was as if he'd been sneaked a copy of one of Mrs. Porter's dreaded essay tests in tenth-grade world history class, and the question I had just posed was the only one printed on the test sheet she had just dropped on his desk. The fragrant whiff of a freshly mimeographed piece of paper swept through me.

The sound of the telephone ringing inside his house interrupted us. Adams braced the sides of his chair, then changed his mind and decreed, "Let the machine get it." After the ringing stopped, he pressed forward, his arms resting on the end of the table. He slid to the edge of his chair. His brown eyes danced; he was busy building his answer.

"Remember that first spring we lived in Maplewood,

when we had Little League tryouts? It was late March, a cold day—full of drizzle, like the second half of March always seemed to be in Ohio. Too wet to play on the baseball fields. Remember? My parents dropped us off at the edge of the shopping center parking lot."

I closed my eyes as Adams spoke and felt the chill he described, heard the anxious, hushed voices of two hundred boys whispering to each other, the sharp commands of two dozen men, the crack of wooden bats hitting balls, the sound balls make when they're speared by leather baseball gloves on cold days. I wondered why the people who owned the shopping center built that parking lot so big. It was never more than half filled, even during Christmas season. The outer edge of the lake of black patched asphalt was so distant from the lights of the stores that it became a destination point for loitering kids who Maplewood's vigilant adults and small police force were sure were up to no good.

The memory Adams had recreated caused me to break into a sweat. "I remember. Somebody's father called your number. It was written in black Magic Marker on a piece of white paper attached with safety pins to the back of your sweatshirt. He hit two ground balls to you."

The balls were rubber-coated, because Maplewood

Little League's Founding Fathers didn't want to scuff the leather-covered baseballs on the parking lot asphalt. The rubber-coated hardball came at you quickly, like a golf ball thrown against a brick wall. It bounced almost as wildly. After you caught the ball or knocked it down, you threw it to somebody's father who pretended he was playing first base.

Adams took up the story again: "Then you were pushed to another line and hit a couple of fly balls. You threw five pitches to a catcher from a makeshift pitcher's mound on the grass next to the parking lot. Finally, you got three swings at pitches from some adult who couldn't throw the ball over a plastic home plate. God help you if you didn't swing at every one of his pitches."

I closed my eyes and recalled the groans from the grown-ups and how louder they got with every bad pitch you didn't swing at. Men with clipboards were constantly evaluating us. They stood in clumps of two and three watching us, talking to each other in hushed tones after every ball was caught, missed, tossed, or hit. They took notes about our performance that none of us ever saw, with the exception of James Roan, a provisional member of our clique who lived on Keats Drive. Roan somehow had access to everything we were never supposed to see:

everyone's permanent record at school, everybody's IQ and SAT scores, *Playboy* magazines, and boxes full of paperback crime novels that featured buxom women in provocative poses on their laminated covers.

Roan even knew all our teachers' first names. But his greatest accomplishment was when he uncovered proof in seventh grade that we were divided into class sections based on how smart the teachers, the principal, and school administrators determined we were. Breech, Adams, and I were in 7B, a class full of kids who Roan claimed had higher IQs than the kids in 7A. Roan was in 7D. He couldn't dribble a basketball to save his life, but his investigative abilities earned him a permanent place on our crew's periphery.

After a thoughtful pause, Adams continued: "Those Little League tryouts were the first time I was ever in a pressure-packed situation. In Maplewood, a boy's social standing during his entire tenure at school was likely determined during those fifteen minutes on that shopping center parking lot. I used to seek out situations like that. I was addicted to the adrenalin. Those moments build and measure your character. Character is the essential ingredient in good, effective leadership."

I always thought character-building had more to do

with how we handled the fallout from the bad decisions we made and jaw-dropping disappointment. Over the years, we've have several friendly arguments about that.

Adams had a good baseball tryout that Saturday morning. He became a steady, serviceable member of our Little League team, Martin's Amoco Oil Dodgers. He moved on to Babe Ruth League and the high school baseball team. I spent two years on the Dodgers' bench and never tried out for anything athletic again.

Without stopping to catch his breath, Adams continued: "There's another one, Tom—the summer between sixth and seventh grade. I had an eye exam as soon as school was out that June. I flunked it and was prescribed those damn glasses." He spoke as if the eye exam should have been as important to me as it was to him.

"I hated wearing glasses, but couldn't see much more than twenty feet in front of me without them. Remember Pamela Drake and how the guys would walk her around to the back of Cambridge Elementary School and she'd French-kiss them?"

I nodded and smiled. Pamela Drake was such a hot topic of discussion that summer that mere mention of her name decades later caused me to recall everything about her, down to the mole on her left foot, behind her big toe.

"Well, it took me until mid-August to create the right situation to maneuver her back behind the school. She and I were sitting on the steps in front of one of the school's back doors. After fifteen minutes, I asked if I could kiss her." Adams paused, took a drink of beer, and continued his story. "She looked at me for a long time. Then she shook her head and said, 'No, I don't think so. You're not my type.' I was mortified. Humiliated! I figured it was the glasses. I was chewing three sticks of Dentyne, so it couldn't have been bad breath. She had kissed all the guys on the sixth-grade basketball team except me by then. So I lost the glasses for five years."

Adams shook his head. "It probably cost me the centerfielder's job on the baseball team, a starting spot on the basketball team, maybe two-tenths of a point on my GPA—until I could afford contact lenses midway through our senior year. But nobody's turned me down for a kiss since."

I couldn't tell if Adams was bragging, or making a joke.

"The Pamela Drake experience taught me two lessons, Tom. The ability to execute a plan with style and panache is more important than having developed a good one in the first place. And it taught me to not ask for permission, but for forgiveness."

Adams flashed me one of his trademark smiles. I was beginning to feel better. Pamela Drake had French-kissed me behind Cambridge Elementary School twice that summer.

"How about a pizza?" Adams rose from his chair. He was already in his kitchen before I could respond.

Adams never did pass the ball back to me. I never had a chance that Thursday to talk about my life-shaping Maplewood experiences. Honestly, I was more relieved than offended. It would have taken me a few more drinks to return to places I'm not sure I wanted to go. Still, I was surprised he hadn't mentioned what would surely have been near the top of my list: the death of Victor Pavletich.

CHAPTER FIVE

As I followed Adams into the kitchen his doorbell rang. He had just opened the freezer door when it happened. The sound stopped him mid-task; it seemed to startle him. He took too much time to process how he ought to respond.

After the bell rang a second time, he gathered himself, frozen sausage-and-pepperoni pizza in hand, and walked quickly toward his front door, pausing along the way to check his appearance in a mirror that hung in the hallway. I don't think he noticed that his reflection was carrying a pizza. He ran his fingers through his hair and straightened his Polo shirt.

I followed him, as I had when Breech had knocked on the front door a few hours earlier. But this time I didn't go as far. I stopped at a place where the hallway gave way to the foyer, a part of the house remarkable for its shiny gray marble floor and wrought-iron chandelier that hung precariously from an open second-floor ceiling.

Adams was clutching the doorknob with one hand and dangling the pizza in the other. His body language indicated that the person who had rung the doorbell, a woman it turned out, was capable of draining all the self-confidence he had just preened for me. I presumed that her unannounced visit wasn't entirely unexpected, given Adams's stop in front of the mirror.

As he opened the door, he blocked my view. I could only see her outer edges: her silky-soft dark-blond hair, her arms around Adams as she hugged him, the tips of her shoulders over which her hair slightly draped, the outline of a grass-green summer dress. She fit Adams perfectly. The top of her head nudged neatly under his chin. A white plastic bag dangled from her clasped hands as she hugged him.

Her arms dropped to his side an awkward instant before he relinquished his embrace. He finally stepped aside, allowing me my first good look at her. The late afternoon sunlight that followed the woman into the foyer gave her an angelic presence. I recognized her. We'd been introduced when I last visited Adams in Minnesota three years earlier. She was his next-door neighbor, Christina Peterson. She lived in the house south of his, on the other side of a thick stand of oak and aspen trees that separated their parallel driveways.

What I had just witnessed persuaded me that this woman had become something more than a neighbor since I had last seen her. I wasn't positive. Never during the three years since I'd met her had Adams mentioned her name. And she was not the type of woman I had come to associate with him since his divorce from Kathy twenty years ago. As Adams grew older, his women got younger. Christina Peterson was somewhere near our age. Her beauty was natural, not contrived or owed to youth. She had tawny soft-looking skin that made her eyes the freshest shades of brown and green. Her appearance exuded confidence.

"Michigan peaches," she said, holding the plastic bag up as she stepped back from him. "You'll like them."

Her voice had a cotton-ball purity to it, soft and absorbent.

"Thanks," Adams mumbled. Then he quietly asked her, "What do I owe you?"

His face was long and his voice sad—out of sorts with the words he spoke. His back was against the wall and he was being consumed by it, becoming ever smaller in her presence.

"You owe me nothing," she answered. She stared at him for a moment. Her expression suggested her gift wasn't really peaches.

Recovering some of his swagger, Adams gently pulled Christina through the doorway and closed the door behind her. "I want to introduce you to the man who's been staring at you from the hallway. This is Tom Walker. Tom, this is Christina Peterson, my friend and neighbor."

His eyes never left her as he made the introduction.

My shoes clicked too loudly on the marble floor as I approached her. Christina had stepped in only as far as the door needed to swing shut.

"We've met before," she said, extending her hand. "It was a few years ago—at one of Jonathan's parties."

"Yes, I remember," I answered as I approached her, eager to see her up close.

"It seems Mr. Adams is the only one here who doesn't," she said. We smiled at each other and shook hands. By now, Adams had wedged himself between the closed front door and Christina, blocking her escape. As she spoke, she gently grabbed his chin, forcing him to make eye contact with her like a mother admonishing her six-year-old. "How are you ever going to grow up to be president of the United States if you can't recall who you've introduced to whom?"

Her gestures signaled that she felt comfortable around Adams. It was apparent that she was hardly in awe of him, like the other women who moved in and out of his life. By every indication, she seemed to be at least his equal.

Adams was still holding the frozen pizza. A wet spot on the back of Christina's summer dress, where he had held her in his embrace, indicated the pizza was in the process of defrosting.

"Would you like to stay for dinner?" he asked, his face naturally framing a familiar boyish grin. That look had helped successfully clear a path through every difficult situation I ever had the privilege of watching him navigate. He held the pizza up for her to see. Moving the melting frozen pizza from one hand to the other, he wiped his wet palm on his jeans.

Christina gave the invitation more thought than it deserved. I had a front row seat at a performance where both actors, the only people on stage, seemed to have forgotten their lines.

"Sorry, I can't tonight, Jonathan. Richard is here this weekend. He's making dinner at my house for six of our—" She corrected herself. "Six of his friends. I have to get back. I wanted you to have these. I know how much you like peaches." She passed the plastic bag to Adams's free hand.

Adams looked like he had just walked out of a grocery store, frozen pizza in one hand, fresh produce in the other. He glanced around nervously for a place to put them. He set them on the nearby deacon's bench, on top of my discarded jacket. Then he looked up at Christina, offering her a shrug of his shoulders.

"Well, I'm sorry. You'll be missed at dinner. But that means more for us, Tom." He smiled and brushed a wayward strand of blond hair behind her ear.

Christina gave Adams a frown that was probably meant for only him to see. Then she stepped beside him and reached for my hand. "I've really got to go. It's nice to see you again, Tom. Make sure you and Jonathan come over to my house Saturday night for a drink or two, or five or six. You have it on your calendar, don't you, Jonathan?"

As she spoke, she gently touched his arms just below his shoulders—a gesture of endearment she apparently felt to be inappropriate just as quickly as she had made it. Christina's hands dropped to her side and she stepped back.

"We'll come to your party as long as Richard's not invited," Adams answered. His impish smile never left his face.

Christina smiled back, slipped past him, and was halfway down the driveway before Adams moved. Her soft good-bye and a gentle brush of his cheek with the back of her open hand hung behind her in the air for just a second, then left his house through his wide open red door and chased her home.

*

I pulled a fresh beer from the refrigerator on my way to the back deck. Adams dallied behind me—first in the hallway and then in the kitchen. Alone again, I moved my chair far enough away from the table to allow a full view of Adams's manicured lawn from beneath the bottom of the top porch railing. Dabs of dusty blue in the clouds were turning pink and rose-colored as the sun crawled closer to the horizon. Adams joined me after more time than it should have taken him to stow Christina's peaches and put the pizza in the oven. He resumed his post at the deck railing and stared out over his field of tall prairie grass. Wind brushed the tasseled tops of the long grass. The breeze split into several gentle gusts that chased each other back and forth across the field. I rose from my chair and took a seat next to him on the railing.

"Christina doesn't know about Monday night, does she?"

Adams ignored my question. That wasn't important. Based on what I had just observed I was beginning to think that maybe Christina Peterson could fix him.

His face firmly focused on his prairie, he started to share parts of himself again. The phone inside rang once more, but Adams had no intention of dashing inside to answer it.

"I'm lonely as hell, Tom. I'm surrounded by nice things and beautiful people. But I get no pleasure from the nice things around me and I'm incapable of maintaining a two-way relationship with the beautiful people. Everything I ever been associated with except you has had a beginning, middle, and end."

Adams craned his neck. He closed his eyes as though replaying a tape in his head of what he had just said.

"I sound depressed, don't I? These are the classic symptoms of depression, aren't they?" He kept his eyes shut while he spoke, like someone trying to absorb pain. But the tone of his voice was unemotional, clinical. The way he had just expressed himself was less a cry for help than a struggle to diagnose his state of mind.

I had to find out why he hadn't taken advantage of what Christina seemed so willing to offer. But before I had an opportunity to launch my investigation, we were interrupted.

A Minnesota Highway Patrol officer appeared at the foot of the steps of Adams's deck. The officer's presence startled us. Seeing someone with a silver badge on his chest, a handgun holstered around his waist, usually signals that something on the other side of ordinary has either happened or is about to. I looked out at the field and prepared to duck.

Adams recovered before I did and walked across the deck to speak to the officer. Adams didn't introduce us, but the state patrol officer acknowledged me with a slight nod of his hat-covered head, his left hand touching its brim in a cowboy way. The officer's eyes drifted from me to the yellow tape above the patio door and out to the place in the field where a bullet had been fired three days prior.

Their conversation was a short one, conducted in hushed voices and ending with a handshake. I couldn't hear any of it from where I was. After the police officer politely said good-bye, he pivoted, as if Adams had commanded him to do an about-face. He walked down the steps and disappeared around the corner of the house.

Adams returned to his seat at the patio table. I followed him there and sat down in the chair opposite his. I stared at him expectantly.

"Fingerprints on the rifle didn't match anything in their database. Serial numbers had been filed off. So I guess the kid had a stolen firearm," Adams said, without looking at me. He seemed bothered by this latest news.

"They want to do a full investigation. They're sure there's a terrorist connection and they're worried about gun-toting Muslims riding around town in late-model Toyota pickup trucks." He was trying hard to inject humor into his update. "We've scheduled a meeting for Monday morning at the police station in Brookfield. The FBI will be there. They're the ones driving the theory about an al Qaeda connection. Federal law enforcement agencies see terrorists everywhere these days." Adams shook his head wearily. "At the meeting we'll decide where this goes next."

Adams drained his bottle of beer. "Please don't mention anything about this at the party Saturday, okay? And I really don't want to talk about it anymore tonight, Tom. Everybody's making more of this than it deserves. Let's give it a rest."

I leaned toward Adams, ready to protest, but he placed his index finger to his lips.

CHAPTER SIX

The pizza was unexpectedly tasty thanks to the several beers and a glass of Scotch we had drunk. Like a dining event at a sidewalk café on des Champs-Élysées, dinner pleasantly languished for hours, until the sun finally disappeared into the woods at the far edge of Adams's field. We critiqued the Cleveland Indians' baseball season, now mercifully concluding, and shared our hopes for the Browns, whose football season had just begun.

It was a conversation boys learn how to make by carefully listening to fathers, uncles, and older brothers. Adams and I had learned to speak sports fluently by the time we graduated from elementary school; I was the prodigy between us. I was famous throughout Maplewood for my encyclopedic knowledge of where professional football players had gone to college, which teams played in every World Series since the First World War, sites of all the Summer Olympic Games since 1896, and a smorgasbord of statistics that measured the extraordinary performances of a variety of world-class athletes. My talent in memory compensated for lack of ability to hit or throw a curveball in baseball, to make a left-handed lay-up on a basketball court, or to accomplish absolutely anything in gymnastics.

Our autumn sports symposium had been interrupted twice, not counting last year's postponement when Adams was off in Iraq: by Maggie's traffic accident sixteen Augusts ago, and the two years Adams spent in the Gilbert Islands working as a middle-aged Peace Corps volunteer. The cancellations in the 1990s overlapped a period when the Indians made it to the World Series twice and the Browns broke Cleveland's heart by moving to Baltimore and becoming the Ravens.

Both of us had lived two-thirds of our lives beyond the confines of northeastern Ohio. We fled hundreds of miles away, in opposite directions. But we never lost a shared allegiance to Cleveland's baseball and football teams.

We'd recently adopted the bad habit of replacing sports talk with dreary discussions about our jobs. Passion for mine had steadily drained since Maggie's death. Adams, engaged in work prone to higher highs and lower lows, began to lose enthusiasm midway through his second term in the state senate, right after he'd earned tenure at the University of Minnesota, and at about the same time he realized he was older than the fathers of most of his students and a few of his girlfriends. It was much easier dealing with life's challenges when we were in our twenties and our focus was: What do I want to be? How do I want this to turn out? Lately, it'd been: Who am I? It surely was that Thursday.

"Business is what we do, not who we are," Adams proclaimed. He suggested we end the outdoor segment of our discussion, and I nodded my agreement. Two empty Scotch glasses and the chill that follows darkness near the end of September in Minnesota were three good reasons to make the move.

On our way to the living room, the phone rang again. Wondering aloud whether it was a telemarketer or a real telephone call, Adams hurried off to his office down the hall in a belated attempt to answer it. I found myself alone in the kitchen and used the time constructively, refilling both our glasses with ice and Johnnie Walker Black.

Adams's kitchen was distinctive in its obvious lack of use. Pots and pans hung too neatly from hooks fashionably positioned over a wood-sided, granite-topped island easily accessible to and from all of the kitchen's appliances. His stove, his oven top, his built-in dishwasher, and his refrigerator looked brand new in spite of being at least five years old.

The women who passed through Adams's life and his kitchen must have loved the place. The obvious financial investment he'd made would give them the false impression that he was the rare kind of man who knew his way around a kitchen, creating good things to eat for a steady stream of guests that populated a phantom, vibrant social life. Its neat appearance suggested cleanliness and order--admirable, attractive qualities. His relationships were of such short duration that their favorable opinions were unlikely to be tested.

Retreating to friendlier, more inhabited territory in the living room, I put our refreshed drinks down on a two-month-old issue of *Vanity Fair* that had been tossed on a glass-topped coffee table. I sprawled across a tan, three-section couch and swung my legs onto a wicker ottoman. Content and comfortable, I looked around me.

The room managed to seem both cozy and spacious. A built-in entertainment center, flanked by two wide walnut bookcases, filled a wall that separated the living room from Adams's master bedroom. His majestic gray fieldstone fireplace stood opposite the longest part of the sofa. The fireplace dominated the room and faced the two-story glass wall that offered easy views of the back deck and surely framed countless exceptionally beautiful sunsets.

I reached for my drink. Two pieces of stapled, coffee-stained copy paper, print-side down, peeked halfway out from the remnants of a four-day-old newspaper. I dug the pages out and turned them over. As soon as I started reading, I knew this was something I wasn't meant to see, but I couldn't put it down. The pages contained a free-verse poem, unsigned and untitled:

> When I am with you I feel an answer to something I asked a long, long time ago
>
> It comes with your soft touch on the small of my back
>
> Your fingers lingering on my shoulder, combing through my hair

Kissing my forehead, my nose, your thumb
tracing my lips

Heat rising on my neck, my face, my head

Standing—my back to you now, you
pulling me in

Your face buried in my hair, your lips
tracing the back of my neck

Slowly pushing down the straps of my top

Your hands on the back of my neck again,
sliding down over my shoulders

Leaning back, my shoulders touch your
chest

I feel your fingers close over my throat

Riding down my shoulders, past my
elbows

Slipping off my fingers, over my stomach

I feel the zipper move down as my skirt
falls effortlessly over my feet

Then you remove my bra, my back still
against you, almost naked

You, fully clothed, the material comforting
against my skin

Finally, your fingers push down my
underwear

They, too, fall slippery down my thighs

I am naked now

And I close my eyes as you turn me
around gently and

Your breath catches in appreciation

My heart is pounding with something
good

Knowing I can give you pleasure merely by
my body

You turn me back around and I feel you
bend slightly as you reach down

Your hands on my calves and then my
knees, my thighs, my stomach

Brushing lightly, quickly, over my chest
and up over my throat

I feel my breath catch and move my arms
back over my head and clasp them around
your neck

Back arched, you say my name

Your hands travel back over my breasts
and linger there

So soft you touch me, I fall back leaning
on you

Softly sounds escape my lips

You take your time with this part of me,
able to discern the perfect touch

One hand travels down my stomach,
between my legs

Softly your fingers touch me there, each
without hesitation, but softly still

I know now that this will be that moment,
the one that everyone lives for

The one that many experience over and
over—that I'd be happy to feel just once

Your hand quickens, fingers skilled, but
imperceptibly so

This time, because I trust you, I allow
myself to let go

The room darkens around me

I feel you holding me up, supporting me as
I collapse against you

I feel my body move in strange, exquisite
ways for what seems like hours,

But is really only seconds

You pull me close, leading me to bed,
falling in beside me

Wrapping around me, kissing my
forehead, my lips, my throat

It is there I fall asleep as you watch me,
watch over me, hands protecting

And we are both peaceful, both you and I
complete in this moment

Full

I reached for my glass and took a long drink. I tried, as best I could, to put Adams's buried treasure back exactly as I had found it.

I finished my drink and went off to the kitchen to make another. Just Scotch this time, liberally poured over melting ice.

*

Adams was standing in front of his fireplace when I returned from the kitchen. He had the cordless handset from his office phone with him, and had found his glass of Scotch. When he noticed me re-entering the room, he did a side-step in front of the coffee table, putting his glass down on top of the stack of newspapers piled on it. As he fell into a chair beside the fireplace, its leather cushion made a squeak then gave an audible sigh as his weight forced out a gush of air that had been hiding somewhere inside.

Adams reached for a pair of reading glasses, somehow buried beneath the newspaper and his drink. He pulled the reading glasses from the pile without spilling anything. He saw me watching him. "What are you looking at?" I smiled back at him and didn't answer. "Another thing I hate about getting old," he complained, as he put the glasses on. He repeatedly pressed a button on the black telephone and a puzzled look came over his face.

"What's the matter?" I asked.

Adams stared at the telephone receiver. "Caller ID says that all those missed telephone calls came from a pay phone. The person who called never left a message, and hung up before I picked up the telephone a few minutes ago."

Adams dialed the number. It rang for a long time. Someone finally answered. I listened intently to Adams's half of the conversation.

"Could you tell me where this phone is located?" A pause followed. "The Budget Inn on Sibley Avenue? You haven't been trying to get a hold of someone at 651-789-6204, have you?" Another pause. "Did you notice anyone using the phone a few minutes ago?"

Adams thanked whomever he was talking to and lowered the handset from his ear. As he put his glass back down on the table a hint of a smile overtook his worried expression.

"Do you think that's Linda calling?" I guessed out loud.

"Maybe."

"Where should I go when she shows up in half an hour?" I asked.

Linda McArthur was striking, tall, and blond. I supposed her to be about forty years old by then. Turning forty would have been difficult for Linda. She was the type of person who measured her worth by beauty that belied her age. She had knocked on Adams's door the first night of a visit I made five years ago. That was the only time I had ever laid eyes on her, but I remembered everything about her. She was the kind of woman not easily forgotten. Regardless of whether a man spent five minutes or five years around Linda McArthur, her look, the smell of her perfume, a lingering sense of how she moved, the foggy sound of her voice—all were details he'd more likely remember than the date of his wedding anniversary.

Linda had seemed agitated by my being at Adams's house that night. Only with a great deal of persuasion by Adams, and my emphatic statement that I was tired from my trip and on my way upstairs to bed did she finally come off his front porch and into his house. He told me the next day that she'd stayed until four in the morning. He mentioned little about what they did or talked about, except how nice it was to hear her voice and run his hands along the contours of her body.

Adams took another drink of Scotch. "I've seen her just three times since then," he said. "The last time was in a shop in Uptown that some woman I can't remember pulled me into. I saw Linda before she saw me. I worried that being in the company of another woman would drive her away from me forever. My relationship with Linda—whatever it is, was, or has been—is based on her having access to me whenever she needs it. When Linda needs me, we do this dance. She initiates the contact, but I have to beg her to jump into my life."

Adams moved the handset from his lap to the coffee table. "When I caught her eye, she gave me an ear-to-ear smile that showed she was happy to see me. I mouthed the words 'Call me.' She nodded, then shifted her attention to her husband. He was too busy flirting with a salesgirl to notice me." Adams's smile turned to a frown. "It bothered me that she was worried he'd seen us."

Linda McArthur had drifted in and out of Adams's world for as long as he'd lived in Minnesota. Three times married and twice divorced, Linda was a character from a nineteenth-century English novel: star-crossed, misunderstood, desperate to make a place for herself in a part of the world that didn't take ambitious women seriously.

I remembered her story. Linda McArthur married young, the day after she graduated from high school.

Marriage was a means to escape a masochistic father and an alcoholic mother. She worked as a receptionist at a law firm, where the constant attention of men with power and money reinforced a notion growing inside her that she had assets that could prove strategic. Shedding liabilities like her truck-driver husband and ordinary wardrobe, she was promoted in twelve months' time to trophy wife of one of the firm's four partners.

Adams had first met her after her second marriage had bottomed out. He was taking a junior college course in Spanish, in anticipation of landing a consulting assignment in Central America. Linda was enrolled in the same class because she wanted to be able to communicate with the help she'd inherited: a Mexican gardener, a Panamanian maid, and a handyman from Guatemala. In truth, the Spanish class was on an expanding list of outside activities she had arranged in order to escape her husband, who had tendencies much like her father's. Linda McArthur was in the midst of a doomed effort to recreate herself. Her plan was to use her beauty, her husband's money, and a few of his friends to open doors. Once inside, she could demonstrate skills that would propel her into a career doing either TV commercials or weather reports on the six o'clock evening news.

The evening after their third Spanish class together, at a coffee shop in Edina, Adams listened intently as she described her hopes and dreams. That night, Linda McArthur grabbed a piece of Jonathan Adams that they both knew she could keep for as long as she liked. His genuine interest, lack of judgment, his openness, and his trusting smile drew her in. He was dangerously attracted to fragile, beautiful women who sought his advice and his attention. None of them was needier than Linda McArthur. Her random appearances in his life were balm to his reoccurring bouts of battered self-concept. He was safe port in a storm and a trusted, passionate partner who helped her temporarily escape her turmoil, the eye of her frequent hurricanes.

Adams took a long drink from his half-empty glass. "There's more to Linda than meets the eye." He must have realized the irony in what he said, breaking into laughter. "All she needs is an opportunity and the encouragement to become who she thinks she can be. My support and her sensuality might have been enough glue to hold us together for a while." Adams smiled and finished his drink.

But as the hour passed midnight, and Thursday blended into Friday, there were no more calls. No one knocked at the door.

Our conversation lulled. We stared out Adams's living room window at the darkness surrounding his house. I stirred what was left of my drink with my finger. Adams glanced over his shoulder at the clock that hung on the wall at the far end of the kitchen.

"Do you mind if we watch the ten o'clock news? I taped it. The senate's budget committee had an important hearing today and I'm curious to see how it's reported. This won't take long. I know how to fast-forward the recording."

I smiled. "Sure."

Adams raised himself from his chair, walked across his living room, and opened two cabinet doors on his bookcase wall. They revealed a thin flat-screen television. He pushed the doors back and returned to his chair, carrying the remote control that had been sitting next to the TV. With an exaggerated effort, he aimed it at the screen, as if the remote were a pistol and he was trying to hit a bull's-eye the size of a dime. "This is where the technology gets complicated," Adams said.

There was no mention of the senate's budget committee meeting. The story was likely bumped by extended coverage of a car chase on I-35, south of Minneapolis. A camera on a helicopter filmed four police cars attempting to run down a stolen BMW. The car chase held our attention. Neither of us spoke until the first commercial break.

Sometime during the weather report, handled by a woman not nearly as attractive as Linda McArthur, I decided to press Adams about Christina Peterson. It had been a long day, but I wasn't tired.

CHAPTER SEVEN

Adams had forbidden me to mention anything about jihad, fatwas, or attempted assassinations. I didn't want to talk anymore about work. We had thoroughly covered the subject of Linda McArthur. I couldn't mention the poem I'd found on the coffee table that I wasn't supposed to have seen or read. Christina Peterson was the only subject left floating in the air.

"Tell me about Christina." I spoke in a voice louder than the Ford pickup commercial that concluded the taped ten o'clock news.

Adams grimaced. He stood up to turn off the television. He stared at me for a few seconds. Then he walked to his book-cased wall and stood there with his back to me, facing his TV's black screen. He reached up to the bookcase's top shelf and pulled out a three-hundred-dollar bottle of thirty-year-old single malt Scotch. I recognized the label from across the room. It was Maggie's father's brand—my annual birthday gift to him. It was the kind of present you buy a person you need to impress but don't necessarily want to get close to.

Adams took two crystal glasses from atop a silver tray that was pushed to the back of the shelf. Holding both glasses in one hand with two fingers, and clutching the blue-labeled whiskey bottle against his chest with the other, he slowly retraced his steps across the living room. He cleared a space on the coffee table and placed the two glasses there. He poured us each a double, no ice. Adams handed me mine, and looked down at me.

"You might be getting more than you asked for."

He returned to his chair and balanced himself on the edge of its seat. He stared at me for a second, then started.

"Tom, at least once a month I have a reoccurring dream about going on a trip—a long trip, probably someplace overseas. In my dream, I'm madly scrambling around, trying to pack at the last moment. I've had plenty of time to arrange things and get ready, but I've put it off. When it's time to go, something happens—I can't find my passport, or I'm at the airport and I've forgotten the plane ticket. I've got to run home and get what I need. I run out of time; I miss the plane.

"I'm sitting in a messy room, all by myself. Clothes are strewn all over, files and desk drawers ransacked in my frantic effort to find a visa, a copy of a report I'm supposed to present, a plane ticket, or my passport. I'm left behind, alone, sitting in the middle of a room I've just trashed. Everyone's gone off somewhere, and I'm home alone."

He stirred his drink with his index finger. "I'm living that nightmare. It seems like I've been having some version of that dream almost every night lately. It bothers me more than my Iraq flashbacks."

Adams caught himself. He tried to grab back his last sentence by tossing a beauty contestant's smile my way. Then his expression turned serious, confused.

"Before I left for Iraq, I hadn't had that dream for months. I think Christina Peterson made it go away. Now it haunts me, and I think she has something to do with the fact that it's returned."

He wasn't looking at me as he spoke now. He gaze was out his living room window.

"I suppose I should count my blessings. As unsettling as the dream is for me, it's better than the other one I have once in a while—me waving at three smiling women driving off in a white Toyota."

I sat up straight and swung my feet to the carpeted floor. I wanted to make sure my friend knew he had my undivided attention.

"I want to be in love with Christina. It's a responsible, grown-up thing to do. She's good for me in a hundred different ways." Adams dropped his eyes to his glass of Scotch and began stirring it with his finger again. "Until lately, I didn't realize how important Christina might be to settling everything down. I daydream about what it might be like to spend the rest of my life with her. Maybe that's partly because I know I can't have her. I'm ready to trade passion and magic for comfort and compatibility. I'll make all the necessary adjustments when the passion fades. If I ever get another chance with Christina, she'll never know the difference when it happens."

He paused and invited my response: "Am I making any sense?"

As I tried to process what Adams had just said, I turned to the darkness beyond his living room window. A porch light showed everything outside. All of it was shades of black and gray and damp. Since we had left the deck, fog crept over the prairie grass, crossed the lawn, and covered the porch. For a moment I wasn't thinking about Christina Peterson. My mind was on the poem hiding under a newspaper on the table between us. I hardly knew Christina, but the poem didn't seem to be something she'd write.

Adams pulled me back inside. "The little bits of time I've been around Christina since I've been home feel like when you stand on the edge of a lake at dawn this time of year. Cold air blows over the warm water and right through you. You can watch it happen. It's wonderfully invigorating." For an instant, he seemed to soak in the feeling he described, but the contented expression on his face soon evaporated. "I didn't realize how much I needed her around until she wasn't there anymore."

I moved from the couch to the floor, my back against the furniture, facing Adams like a child in kindergarten listening to his teacher read a new book. Today's story was Christina's.

Born and raised in western Wisconsin, along the brown, churning water of the upper Mississippi River, in the midst of rolling, grass-covered hills, on a neat, well-kept dairy farm, Christina Peterson's childhood was as different from ours as it could possibly be. While we were attending school half days, because Maplewood couldn't construct school buildings fast enough to catch up with our exploding population, Christina was spending grades one through six with the same sixty classmates in an eighty-year-old brick building twice the size it needed to be. While Adams and I were running away from our past, Christina was immersed in hers, living in a house built at the turn of the last century by her father's grandfather, in a community whose population seemed forever stuck at 2200.

The end of her freshman year at the University of Wisconsin, nineteen-year-old Christina Andersen finally said yes to a proposal of marriage—made monthly since the previous Christmas by a twenty-year-old neighbor who had been her boyfriend since the sixth grade. His case was helped by her unplanned pregnancy. Engaged in June, they married that August. The couple moved to Madison. She dropped out of college. Their daughter was born at the end of December. When Heidi started school, Christina returned to the university part time. The same year Heidi graduated from high school, Christina received her law degree.

Her marriage officially lasted until the beginning of her second year in law school. Jim Peterson never developed a serious interest in fatherhood. But he maintained a strong Midwestern commitment to handling all of its moral, economic, and legal obligations—until he and Christina divorced.

After graduating from law school and passing the bar, Christina worked as an assistant district attorney in Ramsey County, which encompassed metropolitan Minneapolis and Saint Paul. Law bored her. She saved enough money to buy a women's dress shop in Wayzata, and developed two generations of loyal clientele, thanks in part to a wave of prosperity that produced an ever-expanding pool of wealthy and upper-middle-class households in Minneapolis's southwest suburbs. Her business became so successful that it afforded her the time and the means to become one of the best women's amateur golfers in the Upper Midwest. In the meantime, Heidi graduated from Brown University, married her psychology professor, and moved to London.

"Christina's been a part of my life since the day she moved in next door. I've always been attracted to her. But I was afraid that I'd jeopardize our friendship if I tried to take us beyond that. She seemed so comfortable with our friendship. She gave me no indication that I'd have a better-than-even chance at drawing her into something deeper."

Adams put his finger in his glass, swirled his whiskey around, and put his finger to his lips. "I think I fell in love with Christina the week before I left for Iraq. Heidi was back for a visit and they invited me to go across the river to Wisconsin for her parents' fiftieth wedding anniversary."

Adams paused. "While her mother was telling me about Christina's first day of school, Christina gave me a 'What's next?' expression that invited me into every corner of her life. It was a road I've never taken—one that begins with years of friendship rather than a wild night of passion. I was supposed to be off to Iraq in a few days. I'd be gone for at least six months. Good timing, huh?" Adams shook his head and flashed his disarming smile.

Politics had made Jonathan Adams a master at talking in sound bites. He'd developed an extraordinary ability to express complex thoughts and ideas in twenty words or less. His talent often flowed from his political discourse to his casual conversation. But as he talked about Christina Peterson that night, succinctness was nowhere in earshot to be found.

"As soon as I got to Iraq, I knew I wanted to be home with Christina. I missed her a lot at first. I'd look at the calendar and get lonely and depressed, then I'd write her an e-mail or Skype her. But, gradually, with all the craziness going on, and with me at the front end of a long-term commitment that required so much of my attention, I figured it would do neither of us much good to get involved in a full-blown long-distance romance. I couldn't afford the distraction and she didn't need to be burdened by a load of worry because of where I was."

Adams cleared his throat. "A week in Iraq is like a month in Minnesota. Everything is speeded up. The longer I was there, the more difficult it was for me to think about things the same way I'd likely think about them if I were back here. I began to question the depth of my feelings for Christina. I wondered if they might be exaggerated by loneliness and my being stuck in a war zone thousands of miles from home."

Adams was struggling to explain himself. "In lots of ways, I reverted to how I used to be in high school."

I decided I had better join our conversation, regardless of whether I had anything profound to say. Adams needed time to catch his breath and organize his thoughts.

"Does this have anything to do with your compulsion to be absolutely sure a girl would say yes before you asked her for a date? You know—the fallout from your Pamela Drake experience?" I laughed out loud in a staged way, hoping to temporarily pull the conversation away from its gravitas and push it toward something more familiar. "A girl had to have more tolerance than Nelson Mandela while she waited for you to move from first smile to first kiss, let alone anything that might happen beyond that. How many times did one of them ask you out before you got around to asking them?"

Adams laughed. "Some of them gave up and moved on, I suspect."

"I was an important instrument in the first stage of your ritual," I reminded him. "How many cafeteria tables and hallway lockers did you dispatch me to?"

It had been my job to leak news to a girl or her friends that Adams was interested. I was trained to assess reactions and report comments when his name was mentioned or after a staged walk-by. I'd marveled at the amount of information Adams had to assemble and carefully analyze before he moved from thought to action—a process that almost always led his object of interest to eventually approach him and introduce herself.

"You're right. I guess that's the way it usually happened." Adams's face grew serious, his voice soft but firm: "But I'm not talking about arranging a first date here. I'm talking about making a commitment."

At the word "commitment" his expression resembled a baby tasting Gerber's creamed asparagus for the first time.

Adams stopped for a moment and stared out the window again, carefully assembling what he was about to say next. "I've always done badly with women over forty. Until now, I never shared their sense of urgency to stake out a committed relationship."

A line from Jane Austen's *Pride and Prejudice* came into my head: "A lady's imagination is very rapid; it jumps from admiration to love, from love to matrimony, in a moment." My photographic memory often spilled over from the backs of baseball cards to books. I was pleasantly surprised that I had retained some of that ability in my old age.

"That's one of the reasons why I've preferred relationships with younger women. Nothing's forced when you're involved with them. It is what it is—a moment to be enjoyed. You try to string as many of those moments together as you can before she finally realizes you're her father's age and you've run out of things to talk about."

Adams was animated, tottering precariously on the edge of his chair's leather cushion. I was making a substantial effort to follow his tortuous train of thought.

I didn't interrupt him to ask questions. He eventually got back on subject.

"The rush-to-matrimony phenomenon didn't seem to affect Christina. All that dating-women-over-forty stuff was absent from what we were talking about and what we were doing before I left for Iraq. We were as spontaneous as twenty-year-olds. She'd pass the newspaper to me on Sunday morning and say, 'Let's go there Wednesday night.' She'd call me on a cold December day and say, 'Drive me to the Como Park Conservatory. I've got to see green, tropical plants.' We did a dozen things like that. I enjoyed all of them. And I marked each one of them by pushing myself closer to her and letting her into places that had been off-limits for a long, long time."

Adams paused for a few seconds and stared at the carpet. "During my flight from Istanbul to Amman, the first leg of my trip home, I decided to go all-in with Christina. I had two days to debrief and decompress in Amman."

Adams dropped down from his chair and onto the carpet, sitting cross-legged now, at my eye level, on the other side of the coffee table. "The day before I headed home, I took a taxi to the old marketplace in Amman. There are two streets in the bazaar filled with jewelry shops. I found a beautiful green amber stone, a silver antique ring setting, and a jeweler who mounted the stone in the ring—all in one afternoon. I called Christina from the hotel to tell her when I was scheduled to arrive in Minneapolis the next day. I left a message on her answering machine and on her cell phone, inviting her to meet me at the airport and spend the weekend with me at the Saint Paul Hotel."

I shuttered. This would have been Adams's first attempt to contact Christina in ten weeks, and I could sense the outcome.

"I got on the Internet to see what was going on back home that weekend. I bought two tickets online to *Turandot*—her favorite opera. It was opening at the Ordway Saturday night."

A smile filled my face. This detailed information was not absolutely essential to Adams's story, but was just the kind of description he always felt compelled to provide. I was on vacation, but I couldn't stop being an editor.

As Adams continued his story, my smile vanished. I knew this was headed for a tragic ending. Yet there was still a hint of excitement in his voice as he told me what he had planned for the two of them his first night home.

Adams had left a message for Christina at her dress shop before he boarded his plane in Amman, bound for Paris. No response. Her answering machine picked up again when he called her house before he left Paris for Minneapolis. Disappointed that he wouldn't be met at the airport, unsure now of what he was walking into, his plane landed at MSP on a Saturday morning. As soon as he cleared Customs, he called Christina's cell phone. Still no answer. He took a cab home from the airport. He called his legislative assistant, told her he'd be in the office early Monday morning, and that there were two tickets waiting for her and her husband at the Ordway that night.

Every time he drove past Christina's house that weekend, the same strange car was parked in her driveway. Its presence prevented any further action. He never called her or stopped by. He would expose himself to disappointment and rejection no longer. Early the next week, the cleaning lady he and Christina shared told him what he feared had happened. Christina had met someone. His name was Richard Hunter: a businessman, ten years younger than Adams, recently divorced, scion of one of the richest families in Minneapolis. Besides being heir to a flour fortune, he owned the largest real estate company in Minnesota. Adams was familiar with

Richard Hunter; he frequently had business at the State Capitol, and was well-connected with Republicans who worked there.

Hunter fancied himself a swashbuckling entrepreneur, and presented himself accordingly. Adams claimed that his carefully crafted reputation was undeserved. He said Hunter frequently made bad business decisions that were papered over by large infusions of cash from the family fortune. As Adams talked, I thought of Jim Breech and his story about the high school senior who broke all of his scoring records at Maplewood High. I felt more comfortable when Adams shifted his focus back to Christina.

Hunter apparently had Christina in his sights for a long time. As Adams moved so excruciatingly slow, so delicately, to wrap his arms around Christina's life, he failed to sense her loneliness. Hunter gave Christina all his time and all his attention. She soaked up everything he poured on her like a five-foot-five, hundred-and-ten-pound sponge. Because Adams had dropped out of Christina's life without any kind of an explanation for more than two months—between the time Hind, Farah, and Nur were killed and when he had tried to call her from Amman—she figured he had lost interest. Work and distance had pushed Christina away from his center. The death of his friends shoved Christina and everything else in the world beyond his reach. His tenuous hold on his previous life was tethered by a single phone call—the one he made to me an hour after the catastrophe in Mosul.

"Their picture was on the society page in the Sunday *Star Tribune* last week." Adams reached over to the coffee table and rummaged through the newspaper, pulling out the society section. I recognized it. The section he gave me had covered the poem. The two coffee-stained pages had disappeared.

"Hunter made a big contribution to the children's museum where she does volunteer work. That's him in the picture giving the director a check. Christina's standing beside him."

I put the newspaper back on the coffee table. To this day I don't know what he did with the poem.

"The ring is in a box somewhere in my office. Christina didn't get the messages I left for her until the Saturday I got back from Iraq—the same day she and Hunter returned from a week at his second home in Florida. I'm glad I didn't run into them in the airport."

Exhausted, Adams placed his glass on the table and buried his face in his hands. He straightened up. "So that's why I've been acting like my porch is the top of a sand dune in the Sahara desert, it's in the middle of the day, and I'm barefoot. I came back from Iraq a mess. I need some full-time support and guidance to fix me. Christina is the right person, in the right place, at the right time. But she's not available anymore because my bad choices and stupid hang-ups have driven her into the arms of somebody else."

Adams was never the self-confident rebel, the Byronic hero, he projected. He was a non-threatening non-conformist who craved acceptance. Fear of rejection—which most of us learn to rationalize away or live with—was the principal motivator in Adams's life. It served him well and it served him badly. He had never lost an election. The possibility that he could lose one made him an outstanding campaigner and an effective politician, but that same fear caused him to avoid a woman's total immersion into his life, or his into hers.

"Have you told Christina how you feel about her since you've been home?" I asked.

I didn't have to wait long for a reply. It came like a thunderclap after lightning has struck something close by.

"Out of the question, Tom. I can't face more rejection. There's no upside for a move like that. In politics, when you decide to press a point, you never put the other side on the spot unless you're sure how they'll react. The same rule applies here."

Adams spoke with conviction. His eyes squinted and he pushed his lips together, underlining his firm look. Then the tone of his voice and the expression on his face changed. He grew pensive.

"Seldom does a day go by without me playing this over and over in my mind. I can't fix this. I can't make things turn out differently." Adams put his hands on the edge of the coffee table and looked at me sternly. "I expect any day now to see an engagement ring on Christina's hand. When Richard Hunter sees something he wants, he moves heaven and hell to get it. That's how he works. And he wants Christina."

I wasn't as convinced that Adams understood the depth of Christina's relationship with Hunter, or that he could predict with certainty how she'd react to his telling her that he loved her. I remembered how Christina had brushed Adams's cheek with the back of her hand before she fled down his driveway.

"How many chances to fall in love land in the laps of people our age?" Adams asked as he reached for the blue-labeled bottle and poured another drink. I attempted once more to shake him from his depression.

"How can you be sure that Christina is as important to you as you say she is? Are you sure you're in love with her? Why isn't it likely that you might meet someone tomorrow, next week, or next month, and fall more in love with that person than you think you have with Christina?" I asked.

Adams jumped up and disappeared down the hallway. Gone less than a minute, he returned from his office carrying a black ringed notebook. He sat back in his leather chair.

I recognized the black book. He took it with him everywhere he went. Its compartments contained a calendar on which he wrote appointments, a slot for business cards of important clients and contacts, and a small notebook in which he jotted reminders, thoughts, and ideas he'd collect during the day. An alphabetized index of street and e-mail addresses and telephone numbers filled another section. As time and space required, he replaced the calendar, reshuffled the business cards, and refilled the notes section with blank paper. Everything Adams had touched over the years had been either lost, tossed out, or replaced at least once—everything except his black organizer.

Adams pulled a tissue-thin piece of paper from its inside pocket—a page torn from a book. He carefully unfolded it and handed it to me. The thinness of the paper and its small print made its source obvious: It was from a *Norton Anthology of American Literature* textbook—the books we were issued on the first day of English class when we were juniors at Maplewood High. On the ripped-out page was a poem by E. E. Cummings: "somewhere i have never travelled."

"I first read this poem when I was sixteen," Adams said. Then he did a remarkable thing. He recited the poem perfectly, word for word, by heart. I followed the words he spoke on the torn page I was holding. I was moved as much by the passion with which he recited the poem as I was by what Cummings had written. Adams's tone was confident and sure, like the voice of a devout Christian saying the Lord's Prayer. He perfectly captured the essence of every one of Cummings's words. When he finished, he emphasized the point he was making by repeating one of the poem's lines:

> your slightest look easily will unclose me
>
> though i have closed myself as fingers,
>
> you open always petal by petal myself as
> Spring opens
>
> (touching skillfully, mysteriously) her first
> rose

Adams pushed himself back from the edge of his

chair and settled deep into its confines. I was speechless. A thick silence hung in the room before he cut it with a matter-of-fact statement: "This is my yardstick. This is how I know what love is. It describes how loving someone makes you feel about the person you love, and how that love affects you."

Adams extended an open hand to me. The glimpse he had allowed me into his soul was over. I passed the sacred torn page back to him. He carefully folded it and returned it to its protected place inside his indispensable black book.

He had managed to discover the definition of love. He had found a way to identify and measure its feeling and determine its depth and breadth. I wondered what other important things he had kept hidden from the world, and from me.

*

Hardly pausing long enough to allow me to absorb what had happened, Adams completely changed the tenor of his voice. He made a series of announcements as stark and devoid of feeling as if he were the press secretary telling reporters about the president's next day's schedule: "I've got a nine o'clock class to teach in the morning, and I want you to come to it. I have to make a presentation at a colloquium at ten-thirty. I hope you'll come with me to that, too. I'd also like you to go with me to a political meeting I'm supposed to attend up north tomorrow night and Saturday morning. We'll spend the night at the lodge where the meeting will be held. It's a beautiful drive up there this time of year. You'll enjoy it. The Porsche pulls out of the garage at eight sharp. Breakfast is on your own."

Then Adams's voice changed again. "I'm glad you're here, Tom. I can see how much you want to help me through all this. I truly appreciate it. I have to live most of my life in a very public way. I have to look strong, confident, and decisive. You're the only one around me now who's seen my other side. Can you ever know how important it is to me that I can show it to you, trust you, and not be embarrassed by it?"

There were no hugs or handshakes. Adams reached up to the floor lamp that arched over his chair and switched it off. He stood up, walked across his living room, turned right, and headed toward his master bedroom. I propped myself up against a corner of the couch and stared at the fog and the darkness outside. After a while I put on my shoes, climbed the unlit stairway, and found my room on the second floor.

Settling into bed, I thought about Adams and everything that had happened that day. Recalling how much energy and effort I had to expend to try to make sense of Maggie's death was the closest I could come to empathizing with Adams's frustration, his sense of helplessness, his growing loneliness.

Nothing can ever be put back exactly the way it was. Both of us were too far down the road to say what the hell and start over. For reasons behind our control, things often don't work out the way they ought to. This was a hard lesson for us to learn. As children, we white suburban middle-class American kids were taught that if we wanted something badly enough and we were patient, focused, and willing to pay the price, whatever we wanted could always be had.

Jim Breech learned his lesson well. He never left home—in body, or in spirit, or in mind. Why should he have ever wanted to? Maplewood nurtured Breech in ways Adams and I could only dream about. He had easily moved from super-athlete to the community's most successful businessman. Everything Jim Breech needed to know about life, he learned in first grade: Treat people like you want to be treated, stand by your friends, work hard and play hard, and honor your promises. Maplewood's prescription worked for him. He was the closest of the three of us to living the American Dream.

But Breech was not a happy man that afternoon. That untidy fact made me think about what Maplewood's insulation was costing him as he struggled with the discovery that there are limits to our possibilities. Maplewood allowed him little room for the transformation he needed to make. Adams and I chose lives more complicated. But neither our path nor Breech's had led us to where our generation was promised we could go.

I turned on the lamp on the nightstand next to my bed. After a minute spent staring at the ceiling, I surveyed the room. In addition to my bed, a bookcase, and a chest of drawers, the room was filled by a large, four-section window that looked out over Adams's driveway and his front yard. The first evidence of dawn showed in a bank of brightening pink and gray clouds. I got out of bed and walked over to the bookcase.

On its top shelf was a copy of Adams's opus, *Maximizing Local Revenues by Coordinating Land Use and Fiscal Policies*. Adams never talked about the book, except when someone paid him five thousand dollars to do a forty-minute PowerPoint presentation about how to apply its methodology.

I returned to my bed with the book, opened it, and

started to read. I was asleep by the third page.

CHAPTER EIGHT

Adams's Friday schedule was more evidence of his mighty struggle to put himself back together. As he moved through it, he laid bare all of his divergent parts. Everything—the qualities that drew you to him, his self-destructive tendencies—was on display that day.

*

His classroom was small. When tables and chairs were moved across the wooden floor, they produced enough noise to drown out conversation. The intimacy of the place afforded none of the anonymity craved by students who didn't want to be there.

Nothing hung on the bare lime-green walls except a white projection screen in the front of the room and a clock in the back. A gray metal cart with a projector on it was pushed into a corner, next to one of four floor-to-ceiling windows separated by narrow pillars. The class was scheduled to start at nine. The clock above me read 8:55. There were only three people in the room: myself, seated on a narrow bench built over an old, non-functional steam radiator; Adams, disheveled but intent; and a young woman, appealing in appearance, persistent in her view that Adams should reconsider the grade he'd given her on the last exam.

She was fit and wholesome-looking, like a woman on a Swedish tourism bureau travel poster: tall, long blond hair, dazzling blue eyes. Her eyes were so Caribbean blue I could see their color when she would glance in my direction the length of the room away. She did so frequently, trying to figure out who I was—Adams hadn't introduced us. But that was her fault. She hadn't given him a chance. She'd pounced on him from the hallway as he was unloading the contents of his backpack, ten seconds after he had unlocked the classroom door.

She and Adams were sitting side by side, at a table nearest the front of the room. A graded exam she had pulled from an oversized tote bag lay between them. They were deeply involved in conversation, trying to reconcile different definitions of the word "comity." Adams was an advocate for the textbook's version. The appealing young woman was adamant about a more expansive notion of what the word meant. His resistance was melting. The look on his face suggested he didn't seem to mind losing the argument. By the time the clock had struck nine and the rest of his students were rushing into the room, the two of them had split the difference. He added three more points to her exam grade.

The points were more important to her than they were to Adams. I was disappointed that Adams had capitulated. Based on what I heard across the room he was right, she was wrong.

The classroom's small size and the quiet it contained when just three of us occupied it were the reasons I could easily eavesdrop. Its character changed dramatically as the Westminster chimes on the clock tower in the middle of the quadrangle outside rang nine bells. The noise Adams's students made jostling chairs around, greeting familiar faces, arranging books and notepads in front of them on the long wooden tables, reminded me of the purposeful chaos an orchestra makes tuning its instruments before the conductor comes on stage.

In the same way, the room became quickly quiet when Adams stood up from his chair, held the class roster close to his temporarily bespectacled face, and silently took attendance.

Eight oak conference tables arranged in a big rectangle filled most of the room. Twenty-one people, including Adams, occupied all but three of the chairs that were haphazardly arranged around the outside of the assembled tables. Adams's early-arriving student retained her seat next to him. Using the space around her to spread her notebook, laptop, large handbag, and two textbooks, she appeared neither out of place nor divorced from the rest of her classmates. She had a friendly smile that easily drew return smiles from everybody who looked her way.

I kept my place in the back of the room, seated beneath the wall clock. As Adams was about to begin his class, he glanced at me. His look implied a question: Do you want me to introduce you? I waved him off with a slight shake of my head and class officially began. No one had taken particular notice of me.

The Friday morning session was the discussion component of an introductory course in American political institutions. The course was intended for non-majors—juniors and seniors, mostly teachers-in-training who needed four credits in American government to satisfy a state teaching certification requirement. For four credits his students had to attend two lectures and one of Adams's seminars each week. The lectures were assigned to other faculty members in the political science department. Adams managed three discussion sessions every week. He organized his lesson plans around the material that had been covered in that week's lectures.

Almost everyone in the room was there because he or she had to be. Budding social studies teachers, who might someday directly apply what Adams covered in class, were greatly outnumbered by prospective elementary, algebra, and science teachers. Most of his students saw little of relevance in Adams's syllabus.

Dr. Adams used the Socratic Method to teach his class. It tended to unnerve his students and accounted for why the few empty chairs in the room were closest to where he was standing. The popular notion seemed to be that the farther one sat from the professor, the less likely it was that he or she would be called upon. Being asked to answer specific questions directed to individual students exposed them if they hadn't studied the week's assignment. Adams's first query almost always spurred spirited discussion. From the students' perspective, a robust debate consumed time and reduced the possibility that they would be confronted directly with a question they weren't prepared to answer. Adams had explained all this to me during our forty-minute commute from his house to campus.

The class was an eclectic bunch. But it was less diverse than it seemed to want to be. It was two-thirds female, dressed in the uniform of the day. Three styles of blue jeans covered various lengths of everybody's legs. The loose-fitting layered look was prominent among the men. They seemed overdressed, given the unseasonably warm temperature outside. Many of the women wore tight cotton pullovers, the most intriguing of which were not quite long enough to touch the tops of their jeans or cover their faux-diamond-studded navels. Four of the men wore baseball caps: two, with brims carefully bent in semi-circular curves that framed their foreheads; the other two wore theirs backwards. All of the women had hair long enough to be pulled into a ponytail, braided, or allowed to fall unencumbered to their shoulders, except where it was clipped in random strands with tiny plastic clamps apparently only available in two shades of brown.

Almost everybody was white and tan. Two ethnic Asian women and a woman who appeared to be Native

American allowed a claim could be made that the class was multicultural. All of them were young people who had probably just passed their twentieth birthdays. Their gear and their mannerisms suggested they were classic Generation Y types. The iPads, notebook computers, and energy they brought with them into the little room befitted a confident collection of young men and women aware that they were already among their generation's top twenty percent in terms of status, education, and earning potential. How they channeled that confidence while they were in Adams's classroom spoke volumes about them.

True to form, when Adams tried to launch an examination of Congress's war powers, the class quickly transformed his question into a vivacious verbal exchange about political expediency. Criticizing Congress and how it does its business was easy. Anybody tech-savvy was bound to have been exposed to a web-driven analysis of the subject recently. The discussion had the same characteristics as a conversation on a twenty-four-hour cable television news network: voices rising, frequent interruptions, no requirement to substantiate anything being said.

The more closely I tuned into what was unfolding, the more the content of the conversation cast me back to

Maplewood High School. The quality of the discussion quickly reached the shallow depth of the efforts we'd managed in most of my English classes. Our insightful interpretations of literary classics like *The Tale of Two Cities* and *Julius Caesar* usually came from having read CliffsNotes versions the night before. What spewed from our mouths was the stilted language of literary criticism unsupported by inflections that suggested we knew what we were talking about.

I looked out the window, across the campus two floors below, and wondered if our teachers were ever aware of our shortcuts. We surely weren't the first slackers to discover that Classics Illustrated had published a comic-book version of every novel or Shakespearean play we were assigned to read. Our teachers hardly ever asked us to explain, defend, or describe in detail any aspects of what we eagerly borrowed in condensed form from someplace else. It seemed more important to them that we understood plot and setting than character and theme. I smiled. Maybe Baby Boomers and Generation Y are more alike than different.

Theories, assertions, and bad debate technique spread across the joined tables. Like pooling water, they managed to find and fill the lowest places. His students' points of view and the boisterous, disjointed way they presented them smothered thoughtful examination of the esteemed principle of separation of powers. Still, I doubt I would have listened as carefully if they had talked instead about important aspects of the week's lectures. Like Adams's students, I needed to be entertained if I was expected to learn something along the way.

Two spokespeople emerged from among the assembled students. One of them slipped into his remarks that he was the student senate's president. He looked the part of a campus politician and resembled a young Trotsky: bespectacled and goateed, darting dark eyes. He had the loud confidence of someone who had never faced a problem that wasn't solvable. He claimed his leadership position in the student senate had afforded him considerable experience making tough decisions.

"Look, here's how we handled the plastic water bottle crisis last spring. It's relevant to this discussion. We balanced the right of free choice while, at the same time, we addressed an important environmental issue. We stopped the sale of water in plastic bottles at the university bookstore and dining halls, and we got the university to stop using college funds to buy bottled water. But we didn't say that students couldn't carry it around or drink it."

The student senate president postulated that

unraveling an international crisis was a four-step process—the same process he'd applied to the plastic bottled water controversy. "First, you define the issue," he said. "Then, you figure out a way to clearly describe it to outside observers. Next, you identify all the players with a stake in the outcome. Finally, you develop an action plan that addresses the problem and includes something in it for all of them."

He described each step as if he were reading a recipe for oatmeal raisin cookies. I recognized his process. The four steps came from a self-help book that had held a place near the top of the *New York Times* bestseller list for two months last year. The author had offered his manuscript to us, but I'd passed on it, and his agent eventually took it to Simon & Schuster. Ever since I'd made my bad business decision, Maggie's father had found ways to remind me about it.

The student senate president did not reference his source, and a competing point of view was articulated by Adams's Nordic protégé.

"I'm training to be an elementary school teacher, but even I know that whenever a political decision or public policy is made, unintended consequences have to be considered. There's no place for that kind of examination in Troy's four-step approach. A careful, systematic look at all the alternatives, including analysis of how similar situations were handled in the past, needs to be done." To summarize and support her argument she quoted Harry Truman: "'The only thing new in the world is the history we don't already know.'"

A nice touch, I thought.

Her comments inspired a question from a classmate, who referred to the girl as Anna, about historical symmetry.

"A little empathy, lots of respect, and a shared sense of justice should be considered in the policymaking and decision-making processes, too. Troy's approach leaves no room for that," Anna answered.

Her assertions were the same Adams would have likely made, had he joined the debate. The more she spoke, the surer I was that the discussion on how Adams had graded her test was not the first that had involved just the two of them. His influence was all over her.

But the president of the student senate carried the day. Worse, over the next thirty minutes, he managed to forge a consensus. "It's more important to act quickly than it is to act deliberately," he claimed. Anna's Truman quote was matched by a quote he mistakenly attributed to "one of Shakespeare's characters."

"All's well that ends well," he maintained.

The theme of the play he referenced described Adams's love life more than the management of political decision making. Adams's Eliza Doolittle wilted under her student president's barrage of interruptions.

"Define the issue. Explain it in simple, easy-to-understand terms. Identify the stakeholders. Give something to everybody. And do it fast," he repeated.

Anna was out-gunned by someone advocating a weaker position who could talk louder than she could. Her adversary never addressed the issues she'd raised. He flung his talking points around the room until they covered the walls and the tables and hung heavy in the air. The outcome of the discussion was as frightfully fascinating as its runaway dynamics.

"Look, the United States Constitution was written in the 1780s. In order for it to provide almost any useful instruction about how something ought to be done, it needs to be applied in the context of the twenty-first century," Troy Trotsky maintained.

I watched Adams squirm in his seat when his class decided that it was impractical to involve 535 members of Congress in a decision as important as whether or not we ought to go to war. He put his head in his hands when one of his students said the media could handle "the checks-and-balances thing."

Agreement arose among those who offered opinions that Congress was hopelessly dysfunctional and incapable of playing a useful role in the process. His class decided that the president and his advisors should make war policy and all of the decisions associated with it. Matters like going to war had to be considered and acted upon quickly.

Anna was overwhelmed. Adams jumped into the debate to try to save her.

"How do we hold the president responsible if he makes a bad decision? How do we change course before we're forced to deal with the disaster he's created?"

A young man sitting next to the senate president responded: "If the president screws up, we won't reelect him. If we don't want to wait until the next election, or if he's in his second term and can't run for president again, we impeach him."

A few grunts of support rumbled through the room. Buoyed by the favorable response, the student elaborated: "Given the Monica Lewinsky thing back in the nineties, impeaching a president doesn't seem that difficult to do." A third of the class nodded in agreement.

A young man sitting close to me spoke for the first and only time. "If the president's action produced a bad outcome or caused a bad unintended consequence, people probably wouldn't be able to figure that out, because the problem is probably too complex to be explained in simple terms. Besides, the president controls the microphone. Anyway, most people will have forgotten about the issue in a month or two."

The student senate president jumped back into the discussion. "If a tree falls in a forest and no one is there, does it make a noise?"

Half the class laughed. I could almost hear Adams suck air into his lungs through his suddenly wide-open mouth, as if the class had collectively punched him in the stomach.

Anna, Adams's comely education major, spoke next. "I wrote my class paper about Ronald Reagan's presidency. His foreign and economic policies are the source of a lot of our problems today. Hardly anybody realizes the mess he made of things because it can't be explained in two minutes, or in one- and two-syllable words. And even if somebody could, nobody wants to listen. It's old news. My dad thinks Ronald Reagan's face should be carved on Mount Rushmore. And every year that passes, he believes that more and more. So I guess you guys are right."

The color drained from Adams's face. His apprentice had deserted him. Worse, she'd used what he had taught her as her rationale for capitulating.

Adams once confided in me that his passion for teaching was too much driven by his eagerness to work with an audience of malleable minds. He told me he had to work hard at checking his impulse to lead a discussion rather than facilitate one. His body language shouted that he was struggling to suppress his instincts. Lucky for him, he was saved by the bell.

The debate was abruptly ended by the sound chairs make on wooden floors when they're pushed back from a table. Time was up. Class was over.

Most of Adams's students had escaped the requirement of answering a direct question or offering an opinion during the free-range discussion that had consumed the class period. The silent ones gratefully marched out the door and into the hallway, knowing there were only nine more Fridays left in the semester.

Adams and I were the only people left in the room. It was suddenly as silent as an empty warehouse.

"What just happened here?" he asked me across bare tables and scattered chairs.

"All I can think of is my favorite Daniel Moynihan quote," I answered. "'Everyone is entitled to his own opinion, but not his own facts.'"

I shook my head, shrugged my shoulders, and

we smiled at each other. Adams had just bumped up hard against further evidence that he was becoming an anachronism. He laughed out loud as he packed a dog-eared copy of the Constitution and his notes and a textbook into his black canvas daypack. He was a step away from being completely out the door before I could grab my jacket. I hurriedly followed him out of the building and chased him across the quadrangle.

The colloquium at which Adams was scheduled to make a presentation was a good walk across the campus and had already begun.

*

Sorenson Hall was the largest building on the university's west bank. It housed the College of Business Administration and all its graduate studies programs. It was an imposing six-floor gray-green glass box, wedged onto the edge of a bluff overlooking the Mississippi River. The loud echoes our first steps made on the polished gray tile floor as we crossed its sprawling lobby announced our late entrance.

The colloquium had started at ten o'clock. It was quarter past ten when Adams opened one of the lecture hall's double doors and rushed down the right-side aisle of the amphitheater to take his chair at the table in its pit. I picked up a one-page program from an empty desk pushed just inside the room and slipped into an aisle seat in the back.

The title of the event was "A Symposium on American Foreign Policy Since the 9/11 Terrorist Attacks"—so read the canary-colored sheet of paper that I held in my hands. Adams had campaigned hard to be a presenter, and had even written a paper on the subject. But he wasn't officially invited to be a speaker until after a shorter, reader-friendly version of his research paper was published as an op-ed piece in the *Washington Post*. Adams's graduate degrees were in public administration, not international studies, history, or political science. The academicians who organized the symposium claimed he wasn't qualified to talk about American foreign policy. An editorial in the university's student newspaper and a robust national response to his *Washington Post* article forced the university's political science and history faculties—the event's sponsors—to add another chair at the front table.

Thanks to the dust-up surrounding Adams's inclusion on the panel, attendance at the colloquium was twice as large as expected. Three of the faculty members at the head table shifted uncomfortably in their seats and scowled as they watched Adams try to sneak down the terraced aisle to the front of the room without drawing attention away from the session's first speaker.

Adams could only stay long enough for his twenty-minute presentation and the designated question-and-answer period that followed it. He would have preferred to be able to participate in every aspect of the program, but his calendar was full that Friday. He was due back at his campus office by noon to keep appointments he had made weeks before with two of his graduate students.

Adams's presentation was a critical analysis of the tortuous political justification for preemptive military incursions in foreign countries charged with harming the United States or threatening its interests. It was a critique of America's tendency to support despots and dictators because they provide stability, security, and sustainable partnerships. His argument was mostly a moral one, buttressed by historical case studies of good intentions gone badly. In the end, he asked the panel and the audience to consider one question: "If the long look of history has judged our efforts to affect regime change in Latin America and Africa arrogant misadventures and political fiascos, why will history, fifty years from now, look differently at our attempts to do the same thing in the Middle East?"

Adams's *Washington Post* piece had ended with the same question. I leaned forward in my seat, folding my arms on the back of the empty theater chair in front of me, expecting the same kind of thoughtful response his guest editorial had generated.

I was disappointed; so was Adams, judging from a frown on his face that he held for the next fifteen minutes, the entirety of his presentation's scheduled discussion period.

Student and faculty radicals enthusiastically embraced what Adams had said. They painted his presentation as an indictment of America's "endemic imperialistic tendencies—consistently evident in U.S. history since the run-up to the Spanish-American War." All four of the people who offered that opinion used the same phraseology in statements they masqueraded as questions. Adams was afforded no time to respond.

"Let's see if we can get back to the presentation," the session's moderator directed, after the last "questioner" concluded his remarks.

An equal number of conservatives in the audience made opposing assertions. The endorsements from the Left had made Adams's conclusions easy to mislabel and criticize—never mind that the conservatives, like the liberals, had to twist his premise to prove their point.

An old man in the audience wearing a bowtie stood up and raised his hand. Adams pointed to him.

"Your observations are laden with moral relativism and a typical 1960s 'Blame America first' analysis of current events," the man announced. Scattered applause splashed through the audience. The man sat down.

A faculty member from the economics department spoke next.

"Dr. Adams, need I remind you that the world is vastly different now than it was before September 11? Historical lessons don't apply anymore. The United States is in the middle of what's likely to be a never-ending war on terror. That needs to be acknowledged."

One of the tenured doctors of philosophy in attendance questioned whether Adams's academic credentials and job experience qualified him to be taken seriously. She made no reference to his presentation.

No one asked Adams to expand upon his points. I counted seven statements made and no questions asked. After the chairman of the history department ended the morning's discussion and declared the meeting adjourned for an early lunch, Adams wearily climbed the amphitheater's steps.

Outside in the warm sunshine, a hot-dog vendor had his cart set up on the edge of a parking lot, just beyond the extending shadow of Sorenson Hall. Sitting under an old maple tree, my back up against its wide trunk, we ate a quick lunch: two hot dogs, a shared bag of Fritos, and two Diet Pepsis. Cross-legged on the grass, facing me, Adams admitted that he was disappointed that no one asked him to elaborate on the points he'd tried to make in his presentation. Still, he was confident that the theme of his presentation had not been lost in the rarified air of the lecture hall. "I'm fairly sure my remarks will inspire some thoughtful analysis during the colloquium's afternoon session," he said, cautiously adding, "I wish I could be there—just to make sure my point of view isn't misrepresented."

I quietly consumed my food without sharing my opinion. I suspected that his forty-page paper had been scrutinized by his detractors and his supporters like it was scripture from the Bible's Book of Revelation. His words and ideas were just as likely to be used to support wildly divergent points of view as they were to provoke a thoughtful discussion. It was best that Adams not have to witness the free-for-all.

After twenty minutes, we struggled to our feet, placed our garbage carefully on top of an overflowing waste can, and headed off in the general direction of Adams's campus office. Between smiles and hellos to and from students and faculty members, we lamented the morning's happenings.

"There was something important missing from your class discussion today," I said, "and a Grand Canyon full of misinterpretation of your remarks at the symposium. When people make decisions today, do they understand that they need to be accountable for the consequences? Do you think those kinds of considerations play a role in the decision-making process anymore?"

Adams's answer came fast. "Do we really have to be accountable anymore, Tom? Like my class said, we focus on fixing the problem—and fixing it fast. Consequences and accountability only matter when the fix doesn't work."

He paused before continuing. "We've been doing things that way since our Byron's Lane days. Baby Boomers expect to be defined and measured by their job and the social standing it provides them. Both depend on how effective we are as decision makers. It's tangled up in how we're wired. But I agree with you, Tom," he concluded. "There were a lot of essentials missing in both those debates."

I barely heard Adams laugh. He was getting ahead of me. I had to walk faster.

When we were side by side again, he continued: "I'll

bet we'll be able to say these same kinds of things about the conversations you'll be privy to this weekend at the resort up north. By the end of the day, you and I won't have been exposed to anything we haven't seen reported or heard discussed on TV news and radio talk shows. And that's too bad."

Adams looked straight ahead as he walked. It was as if he were talking to the buildings that surrounded us rather than me. He speeded up his walk again, bounding up the steps of the impressive century-old ivy-covered building that housed his office. Barely getting inside before the door he had swung open had closed on me, I ran up a flight of stairs behind him, gasping for air by the time I got to the place where the stairs emptied into the middle of a dark hallway.

My friend had already made a left turn and was ten yards ahead of me, his hand fumbling in his brown blazer's coat pockets for his keys.

CHAPTER NINE

Adams unlocked the door of his second-floor office and bent over to pick up several pieces of mail that had been pushed through the inch-wide space between the floor and the bottom of the door. He stood barely inside the doorway, examining what he held, providing me just enough space to pass by. His office was exactly what I expected it to be—cramped and cluttered with books.

The room seemed barely wider than the space the door consumed. A flat-screen computer monitor peeked out from behind a mound of research papers stacked on top of his desk. Opposite the desk, hard against the room's lime-green plaster walls, were two tall maple bookcases and a well-worn couch that had managed to wedge between them. An orphaned mahogany writing table that held a pile of professional journals and magazines filled one of the corners of the windowed wall. Two chairs—a contemporary black swivel desk chair and an upholstered straight-backed antique that looked like it had been liberated from a nineteenth-century railroad baron's parlor—rounded out the decorating scheme, such as it was. The black desk chair was pushed tight against a big oak desk. It bumped against the processing unit of his desktop computer, half-hidden underneath the desk. The upholstered chair sat at the side of the desk, facing the room's book-cased wall.

Leaves on the branches of a golden oak tree covered his office's lone window. The little bit of light that managed to find its way in filtered through the leaves and had a yellowish taint as it diffused around the room. There was never a need to close the blinds that hung precariously from the top of the tall window frame.

Adams took a seat in the straight-backed chair next to his desk and opened his mail. Shedding my dark-blue blazer, I pushed the wheeled desk chair back from his desk and sat down.

In front of me, half buried behind research papers and ungraded exams, was a framed picture of Lisa Chandler.

Adams had found Lisa Chandler four years ago roaming the university library on a cold Friday night in March. She was what the business of higher learning refers to as a "non-traditional student." Lisa was a thirty-two-year-old undergraduate psychology major.

I met Lisa Chandler during my last visit to Adams's house in Minnesota. She was consumed by equal parts guilt, confusion, and love for two men at the same time. She was beautiful, in a seductively understated way. She had shoulder-length chestnut hair and soft chocolate-brown eyes. She looked younger than she was, a feature I remember she complained about during a long, enjoyable conversation I had with her one evening, as Adams was making a heroic effort to cook dinner for the three of us.

"Lisa's unbelievably insightful about people and what motivates them," Adams had told me while we cleaned up his kitchen after she had left the next morning. "We've spent hours talking about human nature—what makes us be the way we are. She's damn close to perfect, Tom. Every time I'm around her, I want to make love to her."

The Jonathan Adams/Lisa Chandler partnership might have had a nice shelf life except for the problem that she was married—to an oil rigger who was away on a work assignment somewhere off the coast of Indonesia. Lisa's husband was due to return home three weeks after I met her.

The picture of Lisa Chandler was hugely out of sorts in Adams's universe. It was the first time since his divorce that I'd ever seen a photo of a woman in any of the places where Adams lived or worked. Its placement suggested he still needed to have Lisa somewhere in his life, even if all he could hold close to him was a memory of her.

His comments the night before about his feelings for Christina Peterson took on more meaning. Somewhere in his thoughts he was trying to figure out how he might be able to create an environment where Christina could comfortably fit into his life, accompanied the consistent, constant passion he had felt for Lisa.

The picture on his desk put an exclamation point on his Lisa Chandler relationship. Seeing the image of her face in the framed photo recalled the story he'd once told me about how and why it had abruptly ended.

Adams came to New York the day Lisa's husband returned to Minnesota, less than a month after the three of us had had dinner at his house. It was mid-June, and he was dragging me to Guyana to help him on a consulting project he had hastily arranged. The job was an excuse to get out of town. Adams's intention was to come home in July with less baggage than he had taken with him to South America in June. I was there to help him bridge his sense of loss more than I was there to help Guyana develop a method for listing and assessing private property for tax purposes.

Adams never told me what Lisa Chandler had meant to him, but it was clear from his poignant description of how they ended their time together that she was, and would always be, Polaris, the North Star, in the constellation of women who loved him.

His relationship with Lisa Chandler had died here, in his campus office, on a Saturday morning, a week before our hastily arranged flight to Guyana. He told me what happened over gin and tonics at the Pegasus Hotel's poolside bar our first sweaty night in Georgetown. Adams had described the event with such vividness and intensity that I could recall all of its detail that Friday in his office, years later.

They'd sat on the couch in his campus office, opposite each other. Adams was pressed against one end, giving Lisa the space between them he knew she wanted. She was curled up in the fetal position, as far away as she could be from him, her arms crossed tightly against her chest. Her message was obvious: All the places she had allowed him to touch were closed to him now, and would be forever.

In Lisa Chandler's mind she had to cast Jonathan Adams as the serpent in her Garden of Eden. He accepted the role without an argument because it helped her anesthetize the guilt she felt, having invited him into every part of her. He had seduced her into tasting the fruit of the Tree of the Knowledge of Good and Evil. This was the revisionist history she had to create, the picture she had to paint of their short, intense relationship. It was the version of their story that she had to force herself to believe in order to explain what had happened and why it had occurred.

Her soft light-brown hair hung in uncombed strands that had fallen haphazardly on either side of her perfect lips and mouth, framing a face contorted by consternation, but at least as beautiful as when he saw her in the moonlight that faintly lit her bedroom the first time they made love. Adams told me that when he closed his eyes and conjured an image of Lisa— something he said he often did—he would think of her hair, its silky softness, how it would gently tumble onto the tops of her shoulders. Letting her hair down was a sure sign she was feeling comfortable. It was a reliable predictor that another glimpse into who she really was would soon be allowed him.

The more she spoke, the wider the couch and the gulf between them seemed to get. She told him that what had seemed so wonderful during that late winter and early spring had irreparably damaged the rest of her life. She was happily married before her husband left for Asia. She didn't know if she could ever feel that way again. She admitted that Adams helped her see what she could become. She said it was not a nice gift to give someone about to reenter a life in which that kind of awareness causes problems.

As she talked, Lisa's hazel eyes rarely glanced up from her folded arms to his face. Adams had a premonition. The rest of her life passed between them. He saw her continuing to develop into an exceptional person. Where she saw struggle and accommodation at the cost of happiness and fulfillment, he saw Lisa poised to do something special. She was at the cusp of the prime of her life. If she had the will to do it, she was capable of creating her own opportunities to flourish. He was as sure of it as she was sure that it could never happen.

From across the empty space between them, Lisa finally looked at him, bewildered. He was someone she had unexpectedly fallen in love with, the person who had upset her ordered life. She had one week to put herself back together. Her mind and her soul were expanded now. She didn't know with what she could fill the space inside her that Adams's absence would surely create. Lisa told Adams that last day they were together that the best she could hope for now was to find a way to carve out a small, undetectable part of the life they had shared and save it somewhere for her to privately savor. This would be the only way she could cope with the rest of it.

Adams was something she had allowed herself to touch—another kind of life. She was unbound by what she used to believe were her limitations. When her husband left a year before, she promised she would be there for him in body and soul when he returned. Having made that promise before she knew a different way wasn't enough reason to break it. The adjustment that had to be made required her immersion back into a state of ignorance—punishment for her infidelity.

Lisa glanced at Adams across the couch. A pained look came over her face. But he saw another face—eyes wide shut, moaning lips, her effervescent chestnut hair hanging over the edge of his bed as she allowed him to touch those parts of her she now so conspicuously concealed from him: the small of her back, the bend in her legs, the nape of her neck. He'd miss their all-night talks and her insight, her trust, the hundred wonderful ways she would respond to his touch—all the things that made her infinitely desirable.

But Adams knew that the important thing then and ever after was to take the pain away. So he listened intently and tried as hard as he could to understand and accept that everything they had enjoyed and shared had to be pulled up by the roots. Both people sitting on opposite ends of that couch knew the most important thing to do now was push Lisa back to where she used to be. Anywhere else was unacceptable. For Lisa Chandler to choose Jonathan Adams would cause too many people heartache.

I picked up the framed picture and looked at it closely, trying to draw even more of Lisa's presence into the room than the space she already occupied. Adams must have known that my long silence meant I was replaying the episode of their breakup.

"I haven't seen her since," he said softly as he rose from his chair to take the picture from my hands. "She was 'somewhere I have never travelled,'" he said in his quietest voice. "Every moment with Lisa was a gift. She was a wonderful surprise."

Suddenly I knew who had written the poem I'd found.

I got up from the desk chair and meandered through an alley of stacked books and mismatched furniture, making my way to his office window.

People who have been good friends for a long time develop an ability to converse as eloquently with a look as with carefully crafted sentences. When I cast this kind of a glance at Adams, he was staring at an Ansel Adams calendar tacked on the wall above his desk. The picture above the month of September was El Capitan at Yosemite. His mind seemed as far away from the University of Minnesota as he was from the place in the picture. My friend's look betrayed a sense of concern.

Adams realized I was looking at him, like people in cars at stoplights who sense when you glance their way. His expression seamlessly transformed into a smile as he refolded a letter he had opened and stuffed it back into its strange blue envelope. The cause of his concern could have been Lisa Chandler, Christina Peterson, or the contents of the letter. I had neither time nor opportunity to solve that mystery. The shadow of his first appointment crossed the threshold of his office.

"You're welcome to stick around, Tom. But I can't imagine you'd be much interested in listening to ninety minutes of the mundane aspects of researching and writing a doctoral thesis."

I fetched my jacket and patted my friend on his shoulder as I passed by the place where he sat. A disheveled young man was standing in the hallway, just outside the door, awkwardly clutching the draft of a research paper and a heavily book-marked textbook. He was as anxious to get into Adams's office as I was to get out.

*

Minnesota was at the back end of a summer that had pleasantly lingered in the Upper Midwest a month longer than usual. Days like these were always special to those of us in northern climates, and meant to be enjoyed to their absolute fullest. Grassy knolls, lawns, and benches on the campus grounds were full of students desperately soaking in every ounce of gifted sunshine and warm weather.

One of the students drew an appreciative audience as he tossed a Frisbee to a black Labrador retriever that was always able to catch the disc in mid-air. A fraternity brother at Ohio State once advised me that dogs were magnets that attracted women. The scene spread out before me suggested that his theory might still have traction. The young man throwing the Frisbee and his fetching black Lab were about to make new friends. He pointed at two young women intently watching their game, and his dog ran to them and dropped the Frisbee at their feet.

I smiled as I watched. Maggie fell in love with my dog before she fell in love with me.

As I roamed the campus, I struggled to identify the lessons learned from Adams's breakup with Lisa Chandler. Could he apply them to his intense disappointment over his inability to start a relationship with Christina Peterson?

After an hour of aimless walking, I decided there were no lessons to be had. Lisa was his id; Christina was his ego.

CHAPTER TEN

Adams was right: the drive from the University of Minnesota's campus north to the Mille Lacs Lake area was exceptional. The sun, its path across the sky sinking lower with every day that moved Minnesota closer to winter, cast long shadows through the thinning trees and over the road. Intermittent wind gusts caused by cars and trucks moving fast along the two-lane highway made fallen leaves scatter, reassemble, and scatter again across the black asphalt. The landscape all around us was beginning to erupt into a riot of color. The maples were turning red and dark pink; the aspens, gold; the oaks, a dozen shades of amber.

The Porsche clung tight and low to the winding road. Adams drove at his usual pace. We would get to where we were going twenty minutes sooner than we should. We were headed for an upscale backwoods resort, where a political strategy meeting for next year's state legislative campaign would take place.

"You know, I wouldn't have been invited to this meeting if word hadn't leaked to the press last week. I'm the party's trophy wife," Adams said with a smile.

"Is that right?" I answered. "I figured this was an audition for the party's endorsement to be its candidate for governor. But I wasn't going to bring up the subject until we ran out of things to talk about." Adams responded with a laugh.

Jonathan Adams was acknowledged by most people interested in state politics as the conscience of Minnesota's Democratic Party. He enjoyed the moniker, wore it proudly, and seemed to do whatever he could to prove it true. He was often on the short side of lopsided votes in the state senate. He sponsored gun control legislation, controversial tax reform measures, and changes that made the senate more transparent and accessible—televised legislative sessions, liberal referenda laws, tighter registration requirements for lobbyists. He was a frequent guest on local talk shows that covered Minnesota state politics. Any party-sponsored event that would likely be covered by the press had to include him. His attendance gave the events legitimacy and profundity.

Apart from these occasions, Adams and the state government's leading Democrats had little use for each other. Their marriage was one of convenience. They never embraced his *Mr. Smith Goes to Washington* style; he never endorsed the way they did business. But Adams and his party's leaders knew that the public liked to see them dance together. So they danced—and they danced well, especially when microphones sprouted in front of them and the lights on TV cameras were turned on.

"You know, Tom, in some ways, it's easy to be the kind of politician I've always been. I'm like a Republican congressman in the early 1960s. I've never really been in charge of or legally responsible for anything. I stand back, I watch, I compliment and criticize. My proposals have merit and might even fix things, but my priorities and what I think is important are so politically toxic and opposed by armies of lobbyists, the majority of elected Democrats will never touch it."

After ten miles of silence, Adams talked more about politics, and how its hardening edge and increasing dependence on campaign contributions were sapping the fun out of it for him.

"The state party expects me to make at least fifty calls a week to solicit money from donors. I hate the duty. I don't need the money. I haven't had a credible opponent in any of my reelection campaigns. The money I raise pays for somebody else's attempt to get elected. I have no desire to run for reelection next year, just to face four more years of all this."

His announcement, I thought, was caused by his malaise. If he could shed even a little bit of it, he would change his mind. Maybe he'd run for governor. Politics motivated and defined who he was. Women gave quality to Adams's life; politics gave it purpose.

Still, Adams was torn. He didn't know what he could substitute for politics to fill time and keep him sharp. He needed to be in the game. But he was fast approaching a point where he had done just about everything he had ever really wanted on a professional level. He had done well, and mostly on his terms. He was fluttering too close to having to ask himself: Is that all there is? It was a question a baby boomer idealist should never have to ask; we were utterly unprepared to deal with the consequences if the answer was yes.

My life was traveling on a parallel track. My trip west this time was partly business. Minneapolis was on the way to Los Angeles, and I'd be leaving Sunday for what looked to be a week's worth of meetings in California to finish negotiating the sale of Maggie's family's publishing house to a subsidiary of the Disney Corporation. What's Next questions were on my horizon, too. As we passed along the west shore of Mille Lacs Lake we were tantalizingly close to agreement that sometime within the next two years we'd buy a medium-size yacht and sail it down the Mississippi River, across the Gulf of Mexico, to the Florida Keys.

"We'll moor the boat in a trendy marina, live on it, and use it to attract rich, recently divorced women at least ten years younger than us," Adams decided. "After a year in Florida interviewing prospects, we'll pick two out to marry—one for you, one for me. We'll use our money to buy a racehorse and a minor league baseball team and live happily ever after."

My hands reached for the sides of my seat as Adams approached a bend in the road; he was halfway committed to passing a cement truck in front of us. Part of me was listening to what he was saying. Most of me was trying to determine if he was really intending to pass the truck on a fast-approaching blind curve.

"I've thought a lot lately about getting back in the horse business," Adams said, downshifting, pulling his car closer to the back of the truck. "I've actually been thinking about that more than I've thought about getting married again. I've had better luck with horses."

He laughed. I gripped the sides of my seat tighter.

A few years before Adams was first elected to the legislature, the state government passed laws that allowed pari-mutuel betting. A robust thoroughbred horse-racing business briefly flourished in Minnesota. A racetrack was built near where he lived. Some of his neighbors originally moved to the area intending to breed, board, and raise thoroughbred horses for a living. Adams formed a partnership with two of his friends and they bought a gelded yearling, the last son of the famous racehorse Alydar. The father of Adams's horse was a notorious underachiever who made a career of finishing second to Affirmed, a racehorse of lesser stature by every measure, who somehow managed to win the Triple Crown in 1978. The only place Alydar ever beat Affirmed was on the stud farm.

Adams's horse was an accident. His unremarkable mother was in a fenced field she wasn't supposed to be in when Alydar showed up in a frisky mood, despite his old age.

Belying his checkered beginning, for two miraculous years Adams's horse performed like his father was expected to. The horse developed a fierce following in the Upper Midwest and made his owners a fair amount of money. Their wild ride ended when their prized possession broke his right front leg during a workout, the day before the biggest race of his life at Arlington Park in Chicago.

Big-time horse racing died in Minnesota about the same time Adams and his partners retired their young thoroughbred to pasture. Native American Indian tribes were building gambling casinos. A large one sprouted up on reservation land three miles from the track. Slot machines and blackjack were easier ways to gamble than betting on horses. They provided instant outcomes and immediate gratification. Gamblers no longer had to study the *Daily Racing Form*, stand in line to place a bet, and wait for twenty minutes to watch a two-minute horse race. Adams bought his first Porsche with part of his share of his horse's winnings. He invested most of the rest of it in the stock market. He eventually drained his investment account to make a huge down payment on his oversized house.

Adams's second Porsche jumped out into the southbound lane, accelerated with a deep-throated groan and a burst of power, and scooted back to our side of the road—five car-lengths in front of the cement truck and comfortably ahead of an oncoming bus. I relaxed my grip on my seat. As utility poles alongside the road passed by my periphery with the frequency of fence posts, we honed our Florida plans.

"Living with characters like us will provide our new wives with excitement like they'll have never known in their previous marriages. By the time we're broke and they're on to us, they'll be too old to make lifestyle adjustments and dump us," Adams said. We both laughed and continued on down the road.

Adams knew exactly where we were going. He had been there before. It was a favorite destination for Democrats seeking a place to do what they used to do in smoke-filled big-city hotel rooms. This was the great outdoors, a green, environmentally-friendly setting. In the north woods, plotting and deal making seemed wholesome. The place we were headed was a hiding spot known to Democrats in Washington as well as Saint Paul; black-and-white and color photographs of three generations of prominent politicians displayed on a wall at the lodge gave them all away.

The resort's location was betrayed by one small sign, nailed discreetly on top of a mailbox post. An arrow attached to the bottom of the sign pointed down a narrow crushed-gravel road that bisected a dense forest of white pines. At the road's end was a crystal clear four-hundred-acre lake shaped like the big sectional couch in Adams's living room. When the tree-lined private drive reached sight of the lake, it widened out into a landscaped parking lot that comfortably bumped up against the front entrance of a massive two-story log cabin lodge. The lodge was flanked on both sides by six cabins. Each of them had frontage on an elbow of what I soon learned was appropriately called Pine Lake. A stable of horses and a well-manicured golf course provided amenities for guests who wanted more than a place to hike, swim, fish, or canoe.

The small band of Democrats—eleven men and four women, the state party's leadership structure—had the place to themselves that weekend. There were eight vehicles in the parking lot. The tourist season had ended on Labor Day, three weeks before. No media were apparently present. Adams told me that the Democrats inside were probably in a bad mood, upset that they'd have to tolerate his presence, listen to his arguments, and consider his opinions for the next eighteen hours. "If they knew the media wouldn't be around, they probably wouldn't have asked me to come."

Adams and I checked into our guest rooms. We changed into the kind of casual clothes that politicians like to be seen wearing but generally don't wear well. By the time we joined the group they had already convened for their kick-off cocktail hour in the lodge's Great Room. We were half an hour late. A dozen faces took note when we walked in.

The large room was windowless. Its lacquered rough wood décor should have made the place heavy, dim, and gloomy, but the birch logs burning in a massive stone fireplace and soft table-lamp lighting gave the place an unexpectedly intimate, cozy feeling.

Bouncing among small cliques of people scattered around the bar, Adams introduced me to all his comrades—state house and senate legislators and two full-time party officials. They were cordial but seemed a bit edgy having someone from outside their inner circle suddenly thrust in their midst. Whenever the conversation allowed, I assured them that I wasn't expecting to attend their meetings—that I had come for the cocktail hour, the ride from Minneapolis, and the fresh air. Adams pulled me aside and scolded me for setting their minds at ease so quickly. He had mischievously spread a story around that I was a card-carrying East Coast Republican.

Like a barn full of cats nervously flicking their tails, the congregation had been whipped into a state of mild agitation before we joined them. Most of Adams's workmates were naturally vivacious and excitable, but they were unusually animated that late Friday afternoon. Word had leaked about the shooting at Adams's house. Wild rumors buzzing around the room when we joined the group made it impossible for Adams to avoid talking about what had happened. He had no choice but to assemble everybody in front of the fireplace and tell them about it.

"On Monday night, somebody took a shot from the field behind my backyard that hit the side of my house. I was standing on my back deck at the time. As you can see, it missed me." Adams chuckled; nobody in his audience joined him. He recalibrated.

"It was probably a stray shot from a kid in the field hunting rabbits. I'm not worried about it. It's nice to see so many of my friends concerned about my well-being." Adams smiled again. The room was quiet.

Then the state's house majority leader spoke: "I heard the FBI is involved in a big way, investigating the shooting. What's that all about?" He clearly knew the answer. He wanted to measure Adams's response.

Adams's smile disappeared. "Look, Pete, I was a bit

critical of radical Islam in a couple of pieces I wrote after I got back from Iraq. The Feds want to be sure there's no cause-and-effect here. This wasn't some radical Muslim's doing. They're better shots." This time quiet laughter rippled through the room.

As he shared his rabbit hunter theory, the tone of his voice was more hesitant and measured than it had been the afternoon before. The veneer on his bravado was beginning to wear off and reveal streaks of concern. I wasn't sure why. I made a mental note to ask him about that during the drive back to Minneapolis.

His audience's interest was different from mine. I feared harm being done to a dear friend; they felt a direct threat. Had al Qaeda followed Adams to Minnesota? What if al Qaeda tried to stage their next attempt somewhere in the State Capitol? What were the chances of collateral damage—that they'd be the deliberately chosen victims of someone wanting to dramatically, emphatically respond to what Adams had written?

He told me later that he was sure the leaked news had come to his colleagues by way of the office of the state police. He was upset about it. Sensing my rekindled anxiety, he pulled me aside and told me the same thing he'd said at the conclusion of his short talk with the

Democrats: "I'll attend to this on Monday. Don't people have anything better to talk about?"

Between trips to the hors d'oeuvre table, I stumbled into the middle of small groups of intense people. Except for the shooting at Adams's house, every conversation was about public opinion polls, fundraising strategies, and techniques to get out the vote. I heard nothing about governing. There was no Hubert Humphrey, Eugene McCarthy, or Paul Wellstone anywhere in the room, willing or ready to address controversial public policy issues or make hard decisions.

During the drive up, Adams had shared his opinion that Minnesota's Democratic-Farmer-Labor Party had gradually lost its soul over the last twenty years. The Republicans had lost theirs, too, he added. So the net effect was a wash. Both political parties were addicted to big money contributions and obsessed with not offending anyone. The essential skill that separated leaders from foot soldiers in politics these days, he told me, was the ability to determine which way the wind was blowing and where the masses were moving, and to run out in front and lead.

He'd laughed and spoke in a deep robotic voice: "'I must follow the people. Am I not their leader?' I'll bet you don't know who said that."

"Benjamin Disraeli," I'd quickly answered.

Happy hour was winding down. Adams's colleagues decided my presence was temporary and non-threatening. Nobody seemed too interested in me, what I did or where I came from, beyond the usual innocuous, gratuitous things strangers ask each other when they're pushed together at cocktail parties. None of the people I met had a talent for that special kind of inane conversation. No one fooled me into thinking they were really listening to my answers to their perfunctory questions. I found this to be odd among successful politicians. It was a glaring lack of an important skill set. When I eventually made my way back to Adams, I told him so.

He laughed. Aware of the irony in his response, he assured me that they all acted differently when they were talking to constituents and potential contributors—and that they figured me to be neither.

After everybody had funneled into an adjacent dining room for a working dinner, I ambled back to my guest room and changed into sweatpants, a sweatshirt, and running shoes. With the assistance of the young man who had checked us in at the front desk, I collected a ham-and-cheese sandwich and a Diet Dr Pepper. He found me a paddle in a closet just inside the lodge's front door and led me outside to an upturned canoe, which we turned over and moved to the edge of the lake. I thanked him as I put my bag of food on its silver aluminum floor, waved off his offer to help, and pushed the small, short canoe smoothly into the water. I hopped into it just as its trailing half slipped contact with the sandy shoreline. I proceeded to explore Pine Lake, as much as I could of it in the remaining daylight.

The water was dead calm. Breezes blowing near the lake's surface made small ripples that sparkled when touched by what was left of the day's sunlight. The waves showed the ghostly wind's progress crossing the lake and disappearing in stands of poplar, pine, aspen, and birch trees on the far side of it. Besides whispering velvet gusts of wind, the only noise on the lake came from my paddle gently churning the water, and the sound the canoe made as it slowly, deliberately moved across its blue-green surface. The brown, rust, green, gold, and red shades of the trees that surrounded the lake reflected spectacularly in its water-mirror and grew ever-dimmer as the sun started to fall into clouds forming just above the treetops on the western horizon.

Cool air moved over water still warm from a summer's worth of heating. At places on the lake that were already shaded by the trees, small wisps of fog began to assemble. As light faded all around me, the patches of mist combined and formed a tissue-thin gray cloud that attached itself to the water. I paddled the canoe toward the fog bank. As I cut through its wall, I felt the fog's cool moistness on my face. I was reminded of what Adams had said about the way Christina made him feel.

I stopped once in the mist and ate my dinner. The damp cloudy cloak around me induced some deep thinking. I missed Maggie. I wished out loud she was there in the canoe with me. I wondered why someone would want to shoot Jonathan Adams.

Dusk's light had faded away by the time I paddled back to my starting point. I pulled the canoe out of the water, onto a patch of grass. I dropped my empty aluminum can and wadded-up paper bag into a trash can and found an Adirondack chair near the shoreline and curled up in it. Serenaded by loons late to leave the lake, I quickly fell asleep.

CHAPTER ELEVEN

Two hours later, Adams was standing over me. He had a blanket draped over one arm and was shaking me awake with the other. It was dark all around us. Before I could apologize for missing our appointment for drinks at the bar, he pointed up to the heavens.

I had never seen a night sky so brightly lit with stars.

With excitement in his voice, he announced the evening's plans he'd made for us: "Let's do something we haven't done in forty years," he said as I stiffly rose from the chair. Adams turned on a flashlight tucked beneath the folded blanket. He led us along the shoreline and out onto a pier that extended beyond the reach of the lodge's floodlights. A small red light pulsed at the end of it. The dock widened at that point. Twenty seconds later I was standing there, looking out at the blackness. Adams was spreading his blanket out over the dock's wooden planks, damp with evening dew. I felt the moisture the blanket had absorbed as we sat down, but it felt comfortable and familiar.

"I'll bet I'm the first guy you ever brought out here," I joked. I detected elements of his famous grin in the dim light of the flashlight, laid flat on the dock. A minute later we were lying on our backs, our faces firmly focused on the Milky Way and scores of constellations that held up a clear, moonless sky.

Like each of the stars above us, Adams was in a reflective mood. Like theirs, his light that night was generated years before—in a faraway galaxy named Maplewood. In a hundred different ways, we were a long way from Byron's Lane. Yet the moment firmly cast us back there in mind and spirit.

"The world was a very different place when we did this last, wasn't it, Tom? It was easier. Nobody knew then as much as we do now about how things are supposed to work. We felt our way through life back then. A lot of what we bumped up against was new, unpredictable.

Nobody assumed they knew what was waiting around the corner."

I looked for the Big Dipper and pondered what he'd said. His stream of thought carried us backwards.

"Just like this magnificent night sky, our whole lives were spread out before us the last time we did this. How far do you think we've come since then? Or maybe I should pose a more interesting question: How close are we to where we were?"

Adams and I had spent at least one night a week during our fourth-grade through sixth-grade summers in our sleeping bags under the stars that hung over my Ohio backyard—the very same stars that peppered the sky over Pine Lake, Minnesota, that Friday night. The familiar setting caused an avalanche of memories.

Girls we barely acknowledged when we saw them in the hallways or in class when we were ten years old became hours-long topics of conversation those summer nights, as we transitioned from grade school to junior high. We improved our fluency in sports talk. We pointed to satellites and high-flying airplanes that we spied moving silently across the sky. We speculated in whispers whether what we had seen might be flying saucers. We listened to WHK on my transistor radio all night for news bulletins of UFO sightings. Between news updates, we listened to Johnny Holliday play the latest hit songs by the Temptations, Roy Orbison, the Four Seasons, and the Beach Boys. We scanned the night sky for shooting stars. When we saw them we reacted like people do when they watch fireworks on the Fourth of July.

After all the lights had gone out inside my house, Adams and I would climb out of our sleeping bags and stealthily meander along the dry drainage ditch that separated the backyards of houses on my side of Byron's Lane from the backyards of houses on the east side of Scott Drive. Near the north end of the block was Julie Cook's house. Mike Bachman swore to us that he had twice watched Julie's mother slip out of shorts and a tank top and into a nightgown. Mrs. Cook was our consensus pick for best-looking mother in the neighborhood. She was divorced. It added to her allure. But we always seemed to arrive after the bedroom lights were out or the curtains had been drawn. Always disappointed, but always undaunted, we'd eventually slink home to my backyard, crawl back into our sleeping bags, and speculate about what Bachman swore he had twice seen.

When I reminded Adams of our backyard adventures he was quick to fill in some of the details I'd forgotten. Loons on the lake occasionally interrupted us with calls to each other. The loud, distinctive sounds they made demanded that attention be paid to them. They were pleasant distractions to an enjoyable discussion.

It was too dark on the dock to clearly see my friend, in spite of being within three feet of each other. We lay on our backs, two sets of eyes firmly focused in the vicinity of Sagittarius and Orion. The blackness all around us had reduced us to familiar voices. I've been told that to meaningfully converse with someone you must look him in his eyes, but I've always found conversations in the dark to be the most powerful. Perhaps it was because of whom I had shared them with up until then: Maggie and Adams.

"Tom, I've been thinking about the things we talked about last night. Maplewood's been on my mind today. Did you ever read *The Prince of Tides?*"

"Yes," I answered. I reminded Adams that Pat Conroy was my favorite writer, that I had lent him my copy of the book fifteen years ago and suggested he might like it.

"God, I guess you're right." He probably shook his head and made a face. Adams continued: "Anyway, he starts the book by writing, 'My wound is geography. It's also my anchorage, my port of call.' That impressed me when I read it. In some ways Maplewood was a great place to grow up. But the place gave us too much time to think. And we always seemed to have alternatives when we were challenged. We solved too many of life's wonderful mysteries because we had time and space to anticipate them, to plan and prepare. The more I learn, the more I read, the more I see and hear, the more doubt I have about heaven and hell—that anything can accurately be described in terms of black or white, right or wrong, good or evil."

Silence intruded on Adams's thoughts. He took a deep breath. "It's in my best interest to get this Doubting Thomas thing straightened out sooner than later. I don't know how much time I've got left."

He laughed quietly, then slightly changed the subject. "I'm a little bit confused by how so much misery can be perpetrated by people who call themselves true believers. A lot of hateful things seem to be done in God's name lately. I'm sure God isn't too happy being constantly thrust into the middle of our power grabs and the messes we make."

Adams's remarks reminded me of a Lincoln biography I had just finished reading. I told him so.

"Abraham Lincoln was confused and bothered about this same thing during the Civil War. Each side claimed to be acting with God's blessing and according to God's will. But surely God can't be for and against the same thing at the same time. In the end, Lincoln figured that whatever was God's purpose was probably something different than his purpose and Jefferson Davis's purpose."

"Maybe Lincoln's opinion is worth consideration. His opinions usually are," Adams responded. We both laughed. "I wonder what Old Abe would have thought if the Confederates were God-fearing Muslims."

A long pause followed. I ended it with a sermon based on theology I borrowed from American Indian culture: "There's evidence all around us tonight that God's here. He's everywhere, if you want to take the time to look. God's the Creator; he's not the Enforcer. And we're supposed to be the Maintainers. Someone in your class this morning mentioned the concept of historical symmetry, remember? I think that's how God tries to teach us lessons about how to get along. He keeps throwing the same stuff at us over and over again until we finally figure out how to handle it. That's the extent of God's role in the affairs of men. It's not about God taking sides."

Adams laughed. "You know, Walker, you're smarter than you look."

He changed his position on the blanket. He was lying on his side, facing me. I saw his outline in the starlight.

"I'm impressed," he continued. "You apparently know a little about historical symmetry. Not much. Just enough to toss it like a hand grenade into a conversation."

We both laughed at Adams's attempt to release air from a topic that was ballooning into something larger than we were capable of keeping under control. Half a long, silent minute later, Adams was sitting with his legs crossed, pointing the beam of his flashlight toward Mars, high above the tree line on the opposite shore.

"How do we deal with guilt? How are we supposed to handle people we've wronged? How about forgiveness? Is it important?"

I lost myself in the stars, looking for inspiration. I finally formed a response.

"Forgiveness is important to two people—you and the person who was hurt by what you did, or who hurt you. Forgiveness trumps guilt. If you forgive or you're forgiven, guilt goes away. Why should it be more complicated than that? Except in a situation that has legal implications, why should anybody else be involved in absolution? Whose business is it, anyway?"

As soon as these words were out of my mouth, I wanted them back—not the opinion I expressed, but how I'd said it. I sounded like I was reading a contract.

Adams picked up on it. "Well, that's definitive," he

answered. "If I disagree with you slightly, or want to know if what I'm thinking about has legal implications, I guess the only place we can address this subject further is appellate court." We both laughed. "But, seriously, I think you've made a good point." Adams shifted his position on the dock again.

"Tom, I gave Pamela Drake way too much credit for being a major influence on my life. I want to replace her with something else."

"You're allowed," I graciously offered.

"You know what was really memorable? Jim Breech's visit yesterday reminded me of it. I've thought about it a few times since he left." Adams's voice became serious. "It was being part of that basketball team our senior year in high school. I hardly played that season, except those two weeks when the Asian flu benched Breech and three other starters."

Adams scored the only points he made all season during that glorious fortnight of his varsity basketball career when a flu epidemic swept through Maplewood and somehow spared him. He reminded me that Maplewood won three of its four games those two weeks.

"We put the town on the map that winter. It was our fifteen minutes of fame. Free haircuts at the barbershop and free chocolate milkshakes anytime we wanted at the Dairy Queen. Our team picture hung in all the store windows. The farther we went in the state tournament, the more the town, the more the region, the more the state of Ohio embraced us. That was my first taste of the benefits of being a winner and being part of something successful that's bigger than me. It taught me that success shared is sweeter than success individually earned."

Adams paused. "I'm sitting here tonight trying to think of a situation I've experienced since that was similar to being a part of a team of ten boys from a little high school in northeastern Ohio who somehow made it all the way to the big-school finals of the state high school basketball tournament. There are precious few circumstances today that can produce that kind of feeling, Tom. But it's different today. Individual achievements are more celebrated these days. Watch ESPN tonight. I rest my case."

Adams didn't stop; he pushed his point harder. "That's too bad. It's hardly comparable, but that basketball team was the closest I'll ever get to knowing what my father must have felt like being part of an army that won a world war and saved civilization; what my grandfather must have felt after he pushed and pulled and prodded my mother's family safely, intact, through twelve years of the Great Depression. We've not been challenged as a generation until now. We're in the middle of a mess that's going to require a whole lot of shared sacrifice to clean up. It's our generation's moment—it's our once-in-a-lifetime opportunity to define ourselves. And we're squandering it by wallowing in arguments about self-protection, distribution of wealth, and what it means to be truly American—instead of manning up and accepting our social responsibilities and sharing our blessings."

My friend was animated; he was rediscovering himself.

While he turned a few more thoughts over in his head, I picked up his last one and carried it forward a bit. "You're right. Think about the history we lived through. How'd it impact us? Take away the civil rights movement. It didn't involve many white boys like us growing up in the suburbs. What's left for milestones and turning points before the economic collapse in 2007-2008?" I answered my question: "John Kennedy's assassination, the Vietnam War, Watergate, and 9/11."

"They're all catastrophes," Adams noted. "We argue about nuances affecting each of them: what happened, why it happened, who's responsible; we draw no real lessons from any of them—even 9/11."

"I agree," I said. "Our finest hours were the Cuban missile crisis and the moon landing. They're thousand-dollar questions on *Jeopardy* because nobody remembers the details."

Adams was slipping into his professorial mode, seasoned by a political perspective that sometimes salted too much of what was in his head and came out of his mouth. "Those big headline events made us lose confidence in the political institutions we were taught to respect in civics class back in the ninth grade. 'Ask not what your country can do for you. Rather, ask what you can do for your country.' That doesn't resonate much in conversations with my students and my colleagues in the state legislature. We've been celebrating unbridled capitalism and individual accomplishment since Reagan was president. I guess we shouldn't be surprised that it comes at the expense of our collective conscience. Nobody wants to talk about social responsibility."

The lake's quiet swept over us as we tried to absorb what both of us had said. Adams continued, in a softer, fatigued voice: "It's so damn hard to get people to think beyond what's in it for them. It's almost always the case that more of something for some of us means less of it for everybody else. Resources are finite, even in flourishing democracies."

Adams pointed out how difficult it is for a contemporary politician to hold progressive ideals and project Frank Capra-style optimism. "If you're in a leadership position, out there all by yourself, you can't afford to make a mistake. There's such a premium on winning," he said. "Failure has too high a price attached to it these days to convince most of us to take chances."

I butted in. "Always remember, my friend: 'There can be no honor in a sure success, but much might be wrested from a sure defeat.'" I was hoping I might change his Christina calculus or persuade him to rededicate himself to a career in politics.

"Now, where did that come from?" he asked, his astonishment discernible even in the darkness.

"Attribute it to David Lean, Peter O'Toole, or Lawrence of Arabia," I answered. "I'm not sure which one."

Adams asked me to remind him to write the quote in his black book when we got back to the lodge.

"Our free-flowing discussion has produced a sense of urgency in me. It's caused me to acknowledge my mortality," he confessed. He told me that his lawyer had called him last week and suggested he needed to amend his will. Adams asked that I remind him to do that, too. We'd finally become like an old married couple, I thought. I had been assigned a job: remind

Adams of things he needed to do, to record things he thought were important. I liked my new role—Boswell to Adams's Johnson.

"Did basketball and baseball really produce so many life lessons for me?" Adams asked, genuinely perplexed. He knew he could expect an honest response from me.

I theatrically stroked my chin, but I doubt if Adams could see. "It's hard to overestimate their importance when we were growing up," I offered. "All our male role models in Maplewood were anxious to bestow on sports the mystical ability to teach us what we'd need to know to successfully handle every challenge we'd ever face."

"Playing basketball and baseball seemed hardly as important to you as it was to me. You seemed to have turned out okay. How'd that happen?" he teased.

Joke aside, Adams had given me the chance to talk about one of my own Maplewood life-changing moments. I described it in excruciating detail.

We were ten years old. It was the Maplewood Little League championship game. Baseball played at that level is obviously very different from baseball played at the major league level. The bases are closer together in Little League. The distance between the pitcher and home plate is shorter. The game lasts six innings instead of nine. But no one can ever convince me that a major league baseball player in the seventh game of a World Series has ever felt more pressure than I felt that day.

It was the first week in August. Our seasons always ended in early August. We could play a full schedule with a full roster and families still had time to load up their station wagons and go on vacation before school started the Wednesday after Labor Day. Our Martin's Amoco Dodgers were playing the Briggs Hardware Tigers for the league championship. An injury during the game and the Byrd brothers having left a week early for a two-week vacation in Florida combined to throw me into the game in the fourth inning.

Weak players were usually hidden in either right field or at second base. I was the second baseman in the bottom of the sixth and last inning. The bases were loaded with Tigers. There were two outs, and a left-handed batter, David DeMarco, was up. He was a good hitter who almost never struck out. We had started the inning leading 6-2. The score was 6-5 when DeMarco walked up to home plate.

The stands were filled with screaming parents. Sweat was pouring down my face. I looked around the infield and outfield. Most of us were saying the same silent prayer: "Please God, don't let DeMarco hit the ball to me."

I could tell what my teammates were thinking by the frozen looks on their faces and the way they were nervously pounding their fists into their baseball gloves, yelling that stupid chatter before every pitch: "Hey batter, hey batter, swing!"

Our coaches taught us to use the time between pitches to figure out all our options to make a putout if the ball was hit to us. We should consider how many outs there were, how many runners were on base, the capabilities of the batter and the pitcher, the angle and speed of the batted ball. Our mantra was the game's most basic defensive fundamental: know what you're going to do with the baseball before you get it. I tried to do that, but my mind couldn't handle anything beyond my incessant internal plea: *Please don't hit the ball to me.*

Adams was playing shortstop, to my right, on the other side of second base. DeMarco hit the first pitch Keith Jones threw to him. It was a hard-hit ground ball—coming right at me.

God, why hast thou forsaken me?

Everything began to move in slow motion—everything except the baseball. I didn't move. I couldn't—I froze. The baseball found me, hit my glove, bounced off my knee. I was frantic.

Adams had run to second base, ten feet away. Everyone was yelling, but all I heard was his calm voice: "Pick up the ball. Flip it to me."

The runner from first base was almost past me, on his way to second base. I dove for the baseball, grabbed it, and pushed it more than threw it in Adams's direction. His glove speared the ball on its first bounce, an instant before the runner's foot touched second base. The umpire crouching next to me yelled, "You're out!" and signaled the same with the thumb of his right hand. Sprawled face-down in the dirt a few feet from the base, I buried my head in my baseball glove and offered a two-second prayer of thanks.

Whether we got that third and final out at second base before the runner from third base touched home plate was an open question. A dozen screaming Briggs Hardware Tigers parents were still arguing about it after we'd left the field. I don't remember the name of the kid who was running from first to second base, but I thanked God that he was slow.

Anyway, we got the out and we won the game.

Technically, I suppose it could be claimed that I was an important part of winning the championship. It was a terrifying experience. I skipped Little League the next summer, announcing to everyone who could hear me that I was dedicating the spring, summer, and fall of 1961 to getting my star badge in Boy Scouts. Since then, I've involved myself in high-stakes sports the way most American men do—vicariously.

Adams reveled in my story. We analyzed every aspect of it like CIA Kremlinologists used to pour over Khrushchev's speeches at the annual Communist Party Congress in Moscow. At first our purpose was to wring whatever laughs we could from it, as adults do when they recall excruciatingly embarrassing childhood incidents from the perspective of decades of distance. We speculated about what might have happened to the rest of my life if DeMarco's ground ball had rolled through my legs. We decided I would have either turned out to be a homeless heroin addict or in prison for some anti-social thing I couldn't help doing to some poor innocent soul.

After we had laughed long and loud enough to cause lights to be turned on in the cabin closest to the dock, we concluded that both of us had overestimated the influence those kinds of experiences could have on people's lives. We said it, but neither of us believed it.

Finally, Adams and I speculated about what kind of fathers we would have been had we pursued the experience of parenthood.

"Kathy and I had a plan," Adams explained. "We'd put each other through graduate school, then we'd raise a family—no more than two kids. I was still in school when we separated."

"It's the only thing I'd change if I had a chance," I confessed.

"Me, too," he said.

After a few minutes of thoughtful silence, Adams stood up and shined the flashlight on the blanket. It was my signal to fold it up.

We walked back down the pier, along the lakeshore, toward the lodge's lights.

CHAPTER TWELVE

Adams let me drive the Porsche back to Minneapolis the next day. We broke camp at the lodge at eleven o'clock, after he and his Democrats had spent three more hours that morning working through the details of what everyone but Adams thought was a winning campaign strategy for next year's election cycle. The maid woke me at ten, wanting to clean the room, tapping on my door with her key. I had slept through good intentions of jogging around the golf course at sunrise and having a hearty breakfast at nine. I had just enough time for a shower and shave. Adams was standing in front of my door, ready to go.

On the way home, Adams spoke very little about what was discussed behind closed doors at the retreat. He said that the decisions made about campaign strategy and game plan that the group had developed erased whatever doubts he had harbored about quitting politics at the end of his term.

"I tried to persuade them to adopt a campaign theme that acknowledged government's responsibilities in times like ours—a campaign platform that focused on how Democrats intended to address a bad economy and a shredded federal safety net. Everybody else in the room argued that a theme like that had to be accompanied by a plan for shared sacrifice. They decided that the message couldn't compete with the Republicans' sound bite: 'We'll cut your taxes and roll back regulations. We'll make government stop wasting your money.' I tried hard these past two days to rekindle some enthusiasm for teaching, research, and politics. Things sparked, but nothing caught fire."

"You know," I offered, "if you were the Democrats' candidate for governor, you could probably force a public discussion about whatever you want, and structure it however you want to. You're clever enough to figure out how to do that without hurting the chances of Democrats running down-ticket."

"Maybe," Adams responded, barely audible. "But a successful candidate for governor has to have fire in his belly. Becoming governor has to be his passion. Passion for anything's hard to generate right now. When Farah, Hind, and Nur were killed, I disintegrated. What good is it to hope for and build something if you can't protect it—especially when fear, hate, and small minds can so easily destroy it?"

Adams paused. "Something sparked on the pier last night. But whatever it was drowned in black coffee and smothered in oatmeal this morning."

My friend turned in his seat and put his hand on my shoulder as I drove. "Thanks for trying, Tom." He rubbed the side of his face as he continued talking. "Political campaigns these days are high-stakes poker games with just one purpose: to sort out winners and losers. A campaign's objective is to win an election; it's not to provide a venue for debating different approaches to solving problems. Winning's become way more important than what winning provides: a chance to govern."

Adams took a pair of sunglasses from the console between our seats and laid them in his lap.

"I'm not as staggered as I used to be by what I saw after the car was hit by that RPG. But the smell—that awful smell—sometimes it comes back when the news on TV shows a bombing somewhere. That footage is a sanitized version of what happens, Tom: people running around, carrying the injured to ambulances, pushing them onto the beds of pickup trucks. You never see the detached body parts spread all over the street, blood pulsing out of gaping holes in a person, shrapnel everywhere. Last month I stopped in mid-sentence when a medevac helicopter flew by a quarter of a mile away while I was giving a speech in Rochester. After it had moved out of earshot, I couldn't remember what I was talking about."

Adams paused. "I had no business being in Iraq, doing what I was doing. The bad guys had no business being there, either. We were on our way out when I was there. The Iraqi government was pushing us out the door. They outlasted us. If that's how you measure who wins and who loses these kinds of conflicts, they won." Adams unlatched his seat belt, turned toward the backseat, and retrieved his black book from his overnight bag. I was sure he was looking for the name and telephone number of a visually stunning woman to invite to Christina's party that night, but after a while, he closed his organizer and carelessly tossed it over his shoulder onto the backseat.

"Doing what I was sent by the State Department to do in Iraq is just another version of what I've been doing here my whole life. If the last twenty-four hours have demonstrated anything, they've proved that my brand of politics is as out-of-date as carbon paper. If I'm ever going to be able to rebuild, it has to be on a different foundation."

Adams put his sunglasses on. He stared at Mille Lacs Lake as we began our drive along its west shore. "There's such a huge void to fill. Do you know what it's like to have to start life over this far into it? You have to reconfigure how you present yourself—you have to recalibrate everything." His was looking at me now, the wrinkles in his forehead conveying sensitivity and gentleness. "Was it like that for you when Maggie died?"

I nodded. "Yes," I said. "I can empathize with you."

I was lying. Maggie had left me with a lifetime of pleasant memories I could savor anytime I wanted.

"Well, that's it, Tom. That's me, here and now. It's nothing as serious as post-traumatic stress syndrome. It's more like a gut check. I've got the ability somewhere inside me to shake all this off. I need something or someone to pick me up and brush me off and help me bury the wreckage somewhere."

Adams checked the contents of the storage

compartment in the Porsche's console for no reason other than it gave him something to do. The only sound was the wind through which his car was slicing.

"Okay. We've talked about Iraq. We can cross that off the list. But keep an eye on me, Tom. Don't be afraid to suggest ways I can fill the hole."

*

I considered using the time Adams was captured in the passenger seat of his car to force an in-depth examination of the Monday night shooting incident. But the farther we got from Pine Lake and its flock of concerned Democrats, the less timely and on point the subject seemed. Further discussion would likely have given their conspiracy theories more credence than they deserved. Besides, Adams had admonished me not to go there. He was meeting with the police about the incident in two days. On the way back to Adams's house, I convinced myself that the matter was being attended to.

Instead of discussing the shooting, I tried to take us back to the defining moments in our Maplewood history. Jim Breech's visit had plowed up acres of memories, but we had conspicuously stayed away from the corner of the field where the most fertile soil was composting.

As Mille Lacs Lake was disappearing in my rear view mirror, I finally asked: "Do you ever think about the day the farmer died?"

Adams looked at me for a second. Then he turned toward the windshield and watched the dashed white lines in the middle of the road disappear under the Porsche's chiseled front fender. He looked up to the sunroof, reached up and pushed the button that opened it. He kept his finger on the button until the roof had spread open enough that we could feel outside air being diverted into the car. "I haven't thought about it for a long time. You know, that's something we've never really talked about."

Victor Pavletich had owned a small farm in Maplewood. Part of his property bounded Adams's end of Byron's Lane. Shelley Drive and three strands of barbed-wire fence separated his farm, his woods, his pond, and his cows from our neighborhood. Pavletich's southern property line ran almost the full length of the north end of our subdivision. His farm was a prime building site for more houses. But Pavletich stubbornly, steadfastly refused to sell any of his land to the developers. They were fast building homes all around him.

In the fall and spring of every year we lived in Maplewood, Adams's parents and their neighbors on the north end of Byron's Lane and along Shelley Drive would complain about the smell of the cow manure the farmer would spread on whatever patch of his field he intended to plant in corn the next growing season. The fact that he was there first, fertilizing his fields long before anybody who lived in the neighborhood ever made footprints on its adjacent soil, mattered nothing at all to the newcomers. The only relevant fact for them was that, for a week or two once or twice every year, it was decidedly unpleasant to be out in their yard or have their windows open when the wind blew from the north.

Pavletich's farm was Disneyland for us. It offered trees that needed to be climbed, frogs and sunfish and tadpoles in his pond that needed to be caught, and dairy cows that had to be ridden after we'd driven one or two of the unfortunate animals into his woods and dropped onto their wide backs from low-hanging tree branches. The land beyond the farmer's barbed-wire fence was a place our parents forbade us to go, which made it even more appealing.

The farmer, as we called Pavletich, would sit on his back porch all summer long—a third of a mile away from his woods, four hundred yards from his pond. He would watch diligently for any sign of us. When he spotted us on his property, he'd grab a shotgun filled with rock salt, jump into an old dark-green Chevrolet pickup truck, and drive hell-bent across his fields straight for us. Even if we hadn't posted a lookout, the clanging noise the truck made as it bounced across the field and the sound of its engine racing in first gear always gave us plenty of time to escape. Tony Spinello was the only one of us who had ever felt the sting of rock salt on his backside, after having trouble dismounting his cow once. The farmer was ten yards away when Spinello finally hit the ground running.

But the games of chase and hide-and-seek ended abruptly one day in the late summer of our twelfth year on earth, the farmer's eighty-third. Pavletich was at the edge of the woods when four of us unexpectedly stumbled into his presence. Seeing us, the farmer hobbled as quickly as he could to his truck, just a few feet away, to get his gun. Just as we turned to scatter, he slumped to the ground next to the truck's passenger door, grasping his chest with one hand, holding the door handle with the other.

He gasped for breath. At first he yelled. Then he begged for us to help him, as loudly as he could in his gradually muffled voice.

We stopped, turned, and watched him. Steve Wright was already over the hill and out of sight. Adams made a move toward where the farmer lay. The old man was clutching his chest with both hands by then. Greg Kearney ran over to Adams, grabbed his arm, and pulled him in the opposite direction, toward the far side of the woods. Kearney was convinced that we'd caused the farmer's heart attack. We needed to be far away from the scene of the crime, or we'd be blamed for it. I watched Adams and Kearney argue. The farmer did, too. The argument lasted a minute or two. Then we ran as fast as we could from the farmer's faint calls for help.

About an hour later, two police cars and an ambulance, flashers pulsing, sirens blowing, rushed up Shelley Drive. They stopped at a place along the farmer's fence line that was nearest to the place in the woods where the farmer's truck was parked. While kids on bicycles and a few mothers streamed to the spot where the police cars and ambulance were parked, the four of us assembled in Kearney's attached garage. Greg, whose father was Maplewood's mayor, closed the garage door behind us. We huddled in its farthest corner. In the darkness of the empty garage we promised each other to never talk to anyone about what we had made happen.

I'd kept the promise until that Saturday in the Porsche on the ride back to Adams's house.

That day in Kearney's garage was the only time I remember an important decision being made in our group without Adams's participation. He had sat mute on the garage's cold cement floor, his back resting uncomfortably against an exposed wooden stud on one of its unfinished interior walls.

The weekly *Maplewood Post* confirmed three days later the rumor that had buzzed around dinner tables on Byron's Lane: Victor Pavletich had died of a heart attack. James Roan told us the day after the newspaper story was published that the farmer died in the ambulance, on his way to the hospital, more than an hour after we had abandoned him. He was found twenty yards from his truck, trying to crawl home. By the time the fire department's paramedics had gotten to him, the farmer's death was a foregone conclusion. There really wasn't much they could do for him.

Adams was pensive as we reached the outer edges of Minneapolis's northern suburbs. Then he broke the silence: "You're right, Tom. That was a seminal moment in my life. I don't like to relive it, so I haven't thought about it. I learned on Byron's Lane that unpleasant things have a tendency to go away if you ignore them long enough. I'm surprised how often that proves to be true."

He straightened his posture in the Porsche's passenger seat and resumed his fixation on the road's centerline. The next words he spoke were offered dispassionately, after having hung for so long in the farthest reaches of the attic of his memory.

"After dinner that night—the day the farmer died—I told my dad what had happened. My sisters were playing outside in the backyard. My mother was in the kitchen doing dishes and putting leftovers away. That was always the best time of the day to talk to him, right after dinner. He was sitting in his chair in the corner of the living room, by the picture window. He was reading the newspaper. By the time I was halfway through my confession he had folded the newspaper up and dropped it on the carpet next to his chair. I had his undivided attention. That was rare. So I expected a thoughtful response and some good advice, like Ward Cleaver used to give Beaver." Adams laughed. He pushed a button on the console. Cool air rushed into the car from somewhere near our feet.

"It turned out that my father's biggest concern was making sure I didn't tell anyone else what I had just told him. He said that Pavletich was a very old man.

He told me that he would probably have had a heart attack and died that day even if we hadn't been there. My father went on to say that telling people—the police in particular—that I was at the scene when the farmer had his heart attack wouldn't bring the farmer back to life. It would only cause problems and a lot of unwanted attention for my family, my friends, and their families. The whole matter was best left alone. He said, 'Son, during the next few days, you should figure out what you can learn from the experience—then put the incident behind you.'"

As he talked, Adams stared at the cars we passed.

"My father offered no judgment about the fact that I didn't try to help the farmer. And he didn't make any suggestions about what lessons I might learn from the experience. Maybe the lesson was to keep my head down and not call attention to myself when I'm in a tough spot. Or maybe it was to stay away from places where I'm not supposed to be. Anyway, I became a lapsed Lutheran that night. I found out that honesty, responsibility, and accountability are abstract concepts—not pillars of conduct. Maybe that's the lesson I was supposed to learn."

Adams reached up and pushed the button that closed the Porsche's sunroof. He watched the process as intently as if he were dismantling a bomb. "The day my father advised me to bury the Pavletich matter, he ceased to be a role model for me. I pulled away from my family and struck out on my own."

"Struck out on your own? That can be interpreted two very different ways," I noted. My comment produced the first smiles since Mille Lacs Lake.

"You know something, Tom? That was actually my number one defining Maplewood moment. It had to be. I've just buried it so deep it never crossed my mind when we talked about this earlier."

I had no similar story to tell. No one—friend or family—had ever mentioned the farmer's passing. I'd occasionally struggled with pangs of guilt about the incident: the consequences of our response, the moral implications of running away instead of trying to help him. The discomfort it caused was intermittent; it came and went quickly.

We had pushed the matter of the farmer's death into the dim light of a gray autumn day more than forty years after it happened. Maybe we could delete it from our conscience now. Adams was stone quiet the last half hour of our trip. He looked straight ahead. After I turned the Porsche onto his county road, I reached behind my seat, pulled a Handi-Wipe from a plastic covered package, and wiped my hands. I offered Adams the package. He shook his head no.

*

Adams did not want to go to Christina's party. After all, it was Christina and Richard's party—not just Christina's. Until that Saturday night, Adams had managed to avoid the reality of Christina's new life. A mile from home, Adams admitted he hadn't recovered from seeing the picture of Hunter and Christina in the Sunday *Star Tribune*. Having to watch Hunter escort Christina around her house that evening would be difficult.

Adams was the instigator of this series of rotating neighborhood parties. For the last five years, they had become a tradition as celebrated as Thanksgiving dinner by its twenty or so regular participants. When he was home, he never missed one; when he was on the road, the person whose turn it was to host the party postponed it until he was back.

As I turned into his driveway Adams announced that he'd go to the party and he'd put on a good show. He had home-field advantage, he told me. Hunter had never been to a neighborhood party. Given what Adams referred as his overbearing personality, Hunter would probably try to change its chemistry—no doubt with disastrous results. Adams was clinging to a feeble hope that maybe, if Christina had the opportunity to see them side by side, he might be able to plant the seed of a notion somewhere inside her that he was a better fit than Hunter.

Once inside Adams's house, I headed upstairs for my bedroom. I wanted to unpack and change clothes. Adams went off in the direction of his office to check telephone messages and e-mails. He dropped his overnight bag in the foyer.

Within a few minutes I heard him yelling to me from the bottom of the stairs, "Put your pants on, Tom. We're going to take a drive over to the Budget Inn. There's a coffee shop next door. You can pick up something for us to drink while I check for signs of Linda McArthur." Adams had had six more payphone calls from the motel on Sibley Avenue.

Five minutes later we were back in the car, headed down the driveway, on our way to Brookfield. "She must be in a really bad way if she called that often and didn't leave a message," he said.

I hoped he'd find her there. Adams needed a diversion from his Christina Peterson crisis.

It was barely a fifteen-minute drive to the motel from Adams's house. The Budget Inn was on Brookfield's main east-west street, just inside the city limits. We cruised through the parking lot. Adams didn't see a car or a vanity license plate he recognized, but wasn't surprised. Linda's husband would buy her a new car as frequently as the rest of us replace bottles of shampoo. The gold Lexus that she drove when she had last visited Adams was surely long gone from their four-car garage.

We parked next to the motel's office. Adams reached across me into the glove compartment and pulled out a brown leather two-fold wallet. He opened it up and flashed a silver badge at me. "The Minnesota Highway Patrol gives these to state legislators. It's saved me a few speeding tickets," he said. "Maybe the badge will allow me a peek at the guest register. I'll meet you in the coffee shop in ten minutes."

Adams was out of the car before I could unlatch my seatbelt. He disappeared into an A-framed building next to a two-story row of motel rooms. The place was at least fifty years old; its style was vintage 1960s, the colors of its peeling paint pink and teal. I got out of the car and walked across the parking lot, toward the Emporium Coffee House.

The Emporium had an authentic coffee house feel to it. Based on its appearance and its unfamiliar name, I assumed it was a locally owned and operated business. Tastefully laid out, the establishment was a cut above the others in the neighborhood. And so were its patrons. The pleasant smell of fresh ground coffee greeted me as I approached the front door.

Waiting in a short line of people wanting to be seated, I looked out over a roomful of tables, chairs, and customers. They were cluttered in no special way around a brightly appointed open area that spread out two steps below the coffee bar where I was standing. My casual survey of the room abruptly stopped when I discovered Christina Peterson sitting off in one of its corners. She was not alone. The man opposite her, his knees touching hers, was Richard Hunter. I recognized him from the newspaper picture Adams had shown me.

Between them were a partially eaten muffin and two coffee cups. The food and the crockery filled most of their table's surface. He was talking intently to her. In the process of making his point, his right hand found a way through the plates and cups that littered the table and rested on hers. She looked down at her coffee cup and up at his face and nodded in agreement to whatever he was saying.

Christina Peterson did not look happy. But she didn't seem unhappy, either. There was an unmistakable air of intimacy about the picture they made.

A clerk informed me that I was next in line. I ordered two regular black coffees to go—they could be made the fastest. As soon as the drinks were put in front of me and I'd paid for them, I rushed outside, meeting Adams in the middle of the parking lot.

"I don't think Linda's here," he announced. "I looked at a week's worth of registration slips. I described her to the desk clerk. I'm sure he would have remembered her if he had seen her. The phone calls are a mystery. I guess I'll just have to be sure I'm around the next time I get one."

He put his Styrofoam coffee cup up to his lips and frowned as he finished his first taste. "All those blends of coffee, and you got plain black?"

I kept my mouth shut.

*

Near the end of our short drive back to Adams's house, I dutifully reminded him that he wanted to do something about his will. He thanked me for the reminder and told me that he could accomplish what he needed to do in what remained of Saturday afternoon. He asked if I'd graciously give him a couple of hours alone in his office. "I need to follow up on a couple of things and have some checks to write and bills to pay. If I put it off, I'm afraid I'll forget about it."

As Adams opened his front door and led me back into his house, he mumbled something about my Lawrence of Arabia quote. He reached into his carry-on bag, still lying in the middle of the foyer, and gave me his black book.

"I liked that Lawrence of Arabia quote last night. Write it on one of the blank pages in the back, okay?" He turned down the hallway and disappeared into his office.

I carried the Day Runner up the stairs and laid it on the bed in my room. After I finished unpacking, I sat down on the carpeted floor, my back up against the foot of the bed, facing the room's wall of windows. A pen in hand, I slid the black book off the bed's comforter and onto my lap. Trying not to intrude on Adams's business or private thoughts, I turned the pages to the first blank sheet. I couldn't help but see Adams's last entry on the opposite page: "Monday meeting, 10:30 @ sheriff's office—Brookfield. Should I bring UM threat letter received Friday 9/23?"

I wrote the quote about success wrested from sure defeat on the next page and shut the book. I couldn't ask Adams about the threat letter without betraying the trust he demonstrated when he gave me his black book. I wouldn't have been surprised if this was the first time he'd ever allowed it to be put in someone else's hands. I decided that I would wait to ask Adams about the letter until after his Monday morning meeting at the sheriff's office. I'd call him from California and make him talk about it.

Downstairs, the door to his office was opened. I stepped just inside the doorway and put his black book down on the edge of his desk. He looked up at me from his computer monitor.

"Hey, Tom, I've got an e-mail here from Gabe Chance. He's offered me those Cleveland Indians shares again. If I bought them from him, maybe I'd be involved in discussions about how to make the Indians pennant contenders. Technically, I'd be a part owner, right? But, then again, Chance owns less than three percent of the team. I guess I'd be lucky if they sent me the minutes of their meetings."

Adams had met Gabe Chance in graduate school, after Chance had had his *Field of Dreams* Moonlight Graham moment as a brief member of the 1971 team.

Called up from the minor leagues at the end of the season, when teams could expand their rosters, he tore the tendon in his pitching arm warming up in the bullpen during a meaningless late September game against the Baltimore Orioles. Almost thirty years later, when the team's owner took the baseball club public in a stock offering in 1999, Chance used what was left of a signing bonus he had prudently invested to buy a few hundred shares. He refused to sell them and make the same tidy profit all the other shareholders did when the current owner bought the team.

I offered my business advice from the doorway: "Owning part of the Indians is appealing, but it doesn't make any business sense. The stock has got be way overvalued. You won't live long enough to recover your outlay," I counseled.

Adams got up from his chair, laughed, and closed the door in my face.

I instinctively headed for the television in the living room. During the time it took me to walk down the hallway, through a corner of the kitchen, around the L-shaped couch, and past the fireplace, I was oddly reminded that, in my family's house on Byron's Lane, we were forbidden to watch television on Saturday afternoons. It was a strange rule, and the only one my mother ever held fast. It imposed no great hardship on me, especially in late September. I wasn't much of a college football fan, and the Indians had vanished from baseball's American League pennant race by then. I spent most Saturdays up the street with Adams at El Capitan, vagabonding around the neighborhood, or doing the two-mile trek, on foot or by bicycle, to the shopping center to hang out with friends at the lunch counter at Woolworth's. We'd nurse ten-cent Cherry Cokes for an hour so that we wouldn't be told to get up and leave.

When I was a reach away from the remote, I decided that instead of aimlessly flipping through a hundred and fifty channels, I'd spend my time alone with an interesting book that I expected was lurking somewhere on the shelves in front of me. Books were my business, so I wasn't keen on spending leisure time immersed in something dense or significant. I decided I'd look for books full of pictures.

Three hundred books had found a home on the shelves on either side of the television. Arranged by genre, a fourth of them were novels. Almost all the novels were nineteenth- and twentieth-century American classics in hardcover and paperback. Sprinkled among them were books of poetry and Shakespeare. Public administration textbooks and books about government that had escaped from Adams's offices at the State Capitol and the university filled the top shelf to the left of the television. A majority were history books, an impressive collection of mostly American history, including a shelf full of biographies.

My hand followed my eyes, causing me to occasionally pull a book from a shelf and thumb through its pages. My attention eventually settled upon a stack of oversized books pushed into a corner of the lowest shelf. I pulled the pile from the bookcase and restacked it on the carpet. I recognized the exposed binding of the second one from the bottom: our high school yearbook. I eagerly yanked it from the pile. My copy was long lost, probably during a move from someplace to somewhere early in my marriage. Maybe it was thrown away by my mother when she moved to Florida, along with my baseball card collection.

I'd been looking for a picture book. This one was filled with hundreds of pictures of people I knew once—faces I hadn't gazed upon in two-thirds of a lifetime.

Stretched out on Adams's living room carpet, yearbook in front of me, I opened it up to its first page. I closely studied each picture and the captions below them. When I finished the section set aside for our senior class—about half the yearbook—I skipped to the index of names at the back.

My name had more page numbers next to it than I thought it would. I felt good about that, particularly when I compared the number of entries written after my name to most of the rest of the names on the page. When I think about high school, I remember it being about endurance rather than enjoyment. The shorthand résumé next to my name suggested something else. I turned the pages back and forth, from the index to pictures of favorite teachers whose faces I had long forgotten; to sophomore girls I'd dated; to senior girls I had hoped to date, but never had the nerve to ask.

I turned to the first page of the index and found "Adams, Jonathan." It was hard to miss. He had a paragraph of page numbers wrapped around his name: varsity club, class salutatorian, Most Likely to Succeed, National Honor Society, baseball and basketball teams, senior class vice president, student council vice president. I smiled as my finger ran down the list.

Adams had been the vice president of almost every high school organization he'd joined. At the end of our junior year, a week after he had won two separate elections for vice president—next year's student council, next year's senior class—Adams shared with me his theory about vice presidencies. He said he was high-profile and well-liked enough that he could probably run for vice president of anything without much chance of losing the election. His opponents for vice president, when he had any, were usually people of potential, testing the waters. Most kids with a résumé like Adams's would probably have run for president. But the vice presidency, he explained to me, guaranteed him a seat at the table when important decisions had to be made. He could win the seat at little risk, avoiding the trauma of having to deal with losing an election. Inevitably, two months into his vice-presidential term of whatever club or class he was a member, the executive board would be looking to him instead of the president for direction on whatever was pressing and important on the agenda. That infuriated Bob Gundy, Adams's archrival at Maplewood High School, who often held the position of president.

The first blank page in the back of Adams's yearbook was crowded full of quotations, well wishes, and familiar signatures. My eyes were drawn to a quotation printed on the bottom of the inside cover page, falsely signed as Lord Byron, and written in Adams's distinctive handwriting:

> For pleasures part I do not grieve, nor
> perils gathering near;
>
> My greatest grief is that I leave nothing
> that claims a tear.

"Where did you find that?"

I'd been so absorbed in the yearbook that I neither saw nor heard Adams enter the living room. He suddenly hovered over me, like an eagle about to descend on an unsuspecting lake trout. I quickly turned the page. I looked at my watch. More than an hour had flown by.

"Lisa must have pulled it out of some box when she arranged those bookcases for me a million years ago."

I scooted across the carpet and took a seat on the floor, my back up against the sectional sofa, our high school yearbook in hand. Adams sat on the other side of the room, facing his book case wall, in front of the toppled stack of books I had discovered on the bookcase's bottom shelf. He restacked them one by one.

When he was finished cleaning up my mess, he walked over to the couch and sat next to me. "It's been forever since I last looked at that yearbook," he said. "Whenever it was, I remember I was bothered that there was no reference anywhere in it to what was going on in the country at the time. Civil rights protests that used to be non-violent freedom marches were full-scale urban riots. Two of the worst ones were in Cleveland and up the turnpike in Detroit. Vietnam War protests were happening everywhere. Four students were killed by the Ohio National Guard just down the road at Kent State. The women's liberation movement was in full swing. And there's not a hint about any of that anywhere in our yearbook."

I looked up from the book and smiled at him. "Don't be so righteous, my friend. I don't remember anyone in our lily-white, college-bound clique, including you, involving us in thoughtful conversations about civil rights or Vietnam. But I do recall a whole lot of discussion about girls, baseball and football, cars, the Beatles and the Rolling Stones. Besides, some of that stuff you mentioned was old news by the time our yearbooks were published." I laughed. "Our attention spans had atrophied. It's an evolutionary outcome we've passed on to the generations that have followed us."

"You're right, Tom," he finally said. After another moment's worth of thought, he shook his head. "Maplewood did a good job insulating us from all that stuff, didn't it? We were as far away from the east side of Cleveland and the campus at Kent State as we were from Vietnam. We were so insulated that my greatest crisis of conscience was about not giving CPR to an eighty-year-old chain-smoking farmer."

We spent the next hour passing his yearbook back and forth as we shared stories about the people on whose faces our fingers randomly fell. For dinner we reheated leftover pizza in the microwave, ate peanuts, and drank beer. Adams decided that we should be fashionably late to Christina's party.

CHAPTER
THIRTEEN

Adams started looking for something to wear to the party at half past seven. He finally found the right combination of jeans, blue cotton shirt, and tan suede jacket eighty minutes later. I waited for him in the living room for almost an hour. As I thumbed through the *Vanity Fair* magazine that I'd found Thursday night, I realized I had been in this situation many times before. We were sixteen years old the first time he did this to me. It was more fallout from the Pamela Drake experience. He needed to have all the stars as perfectly aligned as possible before he was ready to present himself to a woman. I've spent the equivalent of at least three full days of my life waiting for Jonathan Adams.

*

Christina's front yard was a sea of cars, pickup trucks, and SUVs. Every light in her house was on. The sound of people talking loudly in her backyard and the smell of cigarette smoke wafted over the house and met us as we approached the front door. Adams muttered something about Hunter having invited busloads of his friends to the party. "Very few of mine smoke," he said.

Hunter greeted us at the door.

"Hello, Jonathan. It's nice to see you. Come in. I want to talk to you about tax abatements sometime tonight. Remind me, okay?" Hunter pulled Adams through the doorway by the hand he was shaking. He finally let it go and reached for mine.

"You must be Tom. Christina mentioned you were visiting. Welcome to our party. You're from Massachusetts, right? How about those Red Sox?"

I frowned. I lived in Connecticut and was a Cleveland Indians fan. I hated the Red Sox.

Hunter had answered the door wearing tailored

gray slacks and a black silk shirt. "He's overdressed for a neighborhood party," Adams whispered. Hunter was as tall as us, but his hair was shorter. It was unnaturally dark brown for a person his age; he had no hint of gray. His hair was perfectly combed, like a television newscaster's. I heard Adams's teeth grinding as Hunter welcomed me to "our party."

Hunter took the bottle of wine we'd brought over, announcing he'd take it to the kitchen and open it right away "so it could breathe."

"Red wine should always have a chance to breathe," he said in an instructional tone. As we followed Hunter through the foyer, Adams whispered that Hunter's comment was supercilious. Even people who grew up on Byron's Lane knew that you open a bottle of good red wine and let it sit for a few minutes before you drink it.

"I don't know half these people," Adams said too loudly as we split from Hunter and entered Christina's crowded living room. It was easy to see the half to which he was referring. There were two herds of people in the room. The one on our left was dressed like us. Six hands from the conclave were enthusiastically waving us into their corner. The people on the right side grew quieter when we entered the room. I felt like a yearling at a horse auction.

A living room full of people has always seemed a strange, unsettling sight to me. Taking a seat, as seats begin to be scarce, is like plucking the last piece of chocolate from a box of candy. We learned as children that taking the last piece of anything is impolite. So a place to sit in a crowded living room is always available, in spite of the size of the crowd.

We spotted Christina maneuvering between the two groups. Watching her move back and forth between them reminded me of lacing up a brand-new running shoe. She was exquisitely beautiful that night. Her blond hair was pushed up and pinned into an enticing soft bundle on the top of her head. She was wearing half heels, a dark-green leotard, and an off-white cashmere sweater that spilled over her breasts and hips in a tasteful, seductive way. I added Christina's sense of fashion to the growing list of things I liked about her.

Christina saw us, waved, and came over to greet us. She gave Adams an almost imperceptible shrug of her shoulders and a playful it's-not-my-fault look as she walked up to him. She put her hands on his waist and kissed him on the cheek. "Richard invited a few of his friends."

Her words were carefully delivered. Her tone put miles of distance between the act and her involvement in it. I hoped Adams was sensing all this.

She effortlessly launched us into an enjoyable conversation, and I watched Adams cling tenaciously to Christina's lighthearted banter, often offered at his expense. He seemed to like being teased by her.

We had Christina to ourselves for all of five minutes. We took no notice that Hunter had returned from his lair in the kitchen. He was quickly on us, like a lion pounces on an unsuspecting impala.

"May I borrow her?" Hunter's question was really a statement. "Christina, there are some people over here who want to meet you." Maneuvering behind her, Hunter put his hands on her hips and gently pushed her toward his friends on the other side of the room.

"I'll be right back," she told us, in soft defiance, as she looked at us over her shoulder. It didn't happen.

Adams was gobbled up by his gaggle of friends. I spent my time engaged in short bursts of chat with a constant stream of people who cheerily introduced themselves to me. I met no one from Hunter's group; for the most part, they stayed camped in their corner of the living room. But I met all of Adams's neighbors: professional people, a retired couple, and, my favorite, a farmer-turned-writer. He knew better than to try to monopolize my time after he discovered I ran a book publishing business. For his restraint and pleasantry, I gave the man one of my business cards and suggested he send me something he'd written.

I also took the time to wander around Christina's house and stealthily observing her from the edge of her hallway. Both Adams and Christina had become hopelessly stuck in the noisy, crowded living room, as far apart from each other as Hunter could keep them.

There was little evidence of Hunter's presence in Christina's house; from the hallway I could see a pair of his tennis shoes on her bedroom rug, and one of his sweaters on top of a dresser next to her bedroom's open door. No pictures of him or them were anywhere in easy view; no reference hung from magnets on her refrigerator.

Unlike Adams's house, Christina's walls were filled with framed photographs that competed for space with displays of art. Especially interesting was a gallery that filled a wall in her hallway. The photo arrangement consisted of seven pictures. They were all of Christina at various stages in her life: three of her as a child; one that I guessed was her high school graduation picture; she and her daughter; a posed portrait of Christina standing in an English garden; an eight-by-ten picture of her leaning against the rail of a ferryboat, the distinctive skyline of San Francisco in the background. As I looked closely at the pictures, from over my shoulder came a familiar voice. "I took that one," Adams whispered. By the time I turned around, he was halfway to the living room.

I stopped at the makeshift bar in the kitchen and poured myself a glass of Adams's Shiraz. When I reached the end of the hallway, Adams's friends had already pushed him into their corner of the living room. Engaged in an animated conversation with two of his neighbors, he picked up and put down a bottle of beer on Christina's fireplace mantle. From my strategic position in the living room's wide, arched entryway, my eyes sought Christina Peterson. I found her sitting on the carpeted floor, cater-cornered from the place where Adams was standing. Her back leaned up against a couch. Her left hand held a half-empty glass of wine. Her free arm rested on Hunter's knee. He was sitting on the couch behind her. One of his hands was on her shoulders as he spoke in his coffee-shop earnest way to a man sitting next to him.

Christina gazed across her crowded living room. She found Adams. His eyes caught the look that Christina threw his way. It was longer than a glance, shorter than a stare, and it was quickly acknowledged by his smile. She took her arm from Hunter's knee and secretly shook her finger at Adams. Her gesture caused both of his hands to cover his mouth, a mock acknowledgment that he had been caught doing something wrong. He lifted his bottle of beer from its place on the mantle. In an exaggerated way, he wiped off a moisture ring the bottle had never created on its painted surface. His response caused both their smiles to bloom into full-face grins. Conversations in which they each were supposed to be involved swept over the moment. It was gone forever.

The time was right to kidnap Christina. I made my way over to the place where she sat. I offered my hand to her and tossed at Richard Hunter the same request he had made to Adams and me an hour before: "May I borrow her?" Hunter hardly noticed. He was busy making an important point to the man sitting next to him on the couch.

Barely touching her offered hand, I pulled her up from the floor. Standing, smiling, she led me outside, across her patio and a grassy patch of backyard, to the two empty chairs on her studio's tiny porch. The small cottage straddled the edge of her lawn. The place was enchanting—a personification of all I hoped she would be. Built into one of its short walls was a jammed trophy case that testified to her abilities as a golfer. I smiled. Christina displayed her trophies in a private place, hidden from the view of her visitors. A drawing table stood in its far corner. A turntable and speaker box shared space with a stack of old record albums on a deep shelf built into the far wall. Behind and beside the studio was a pond flanked by woods. The place was as far removed from the party as Christina could take me.

As soon as we were seated on the porch's white wicker chairs, she spoke. Her voice was so velvet and soft that it caused me to bend closer so I could better absorb its melody.

"Thanks for rescuing me, Tom. How's Jonathan doing? Is he okay?"

Her question caught me off-guard. It told me that she had sensed the struggle inside Adams that he had tried so hard to hide from her.

"So you know he's having a hard time adjusting to your situation?" I asked. I caught myself stammering. She ignored my question and surprised me with another.

"Tom, one of the neighbors told me someone tried to shoot Jonathan Monday night. What's going on?"

I stammered some more as I offered her Adams's explanation of the incident. Though Adams had requested that I not mention anything about what had happened, I couldn't deny that it had occurred. I had heard no reference to the shooting in any of the conversations I had flitted into at the party. That surprised me; I doubted that police cars in Adams's driveway and men with flashlights scouring his field in the evening darkness had gone unnoticed. Large houses spread over the hills and fields in that area like a mild infestation of dandelions on a suburban lawn. Most of them afforded easy views of his property.

"That's kind of what Jonathan told me," she said after I had finished. "I only had a minute to talk with him about it in the kitchen. Do you really believe that's what happened, Tom? What's being done about it?"

I told Christina about his meeting at the sheriff's office scheduled for the following Monday. I didn't mention the FBI's involvement. I described Adams's apparent indifference to the matter to dull her worry. I told her that the police were keeping a close eye on his house until they figured out what happened. Christina wasn't satisfied with my assurances, but moved on, having convinced herself, like I had, that everything that could be done to protect Adams was in various stages of progress.

Darkness covered the studio's porch and hid us from the rest of the party. From our vantage point, we had a clear view into Christina's house through its huge picture window. The whole lighted living room and all that was happening in it spread out in front of us like a movie on a big screen at a drive-in theater. Adams was pried into a near corner of the room, everybody within hearing distance looking at him. It was a scene with which I was familiar. People were interested in what he was doing, what he was saying, where he had been, and where he was planning to go next. There always seemed to be a discernible hum in the air around Jonathan Adams. Rumors swirled in his wake. I wondered why my friend could never seem to sense his charisma. All he needed was a whiff of it to blow away persistent self-doubt and constant fear of rejection. If only he could see what we all saw.

"I miss Jonathan," Christina sighed. Her eyes never left him as she spoke. "He's been a good friend—a very good friend. But a woman involved with another man can't have best friends—even good friends—who are men. I find that to be grossly unfair, but everyone tells me that that's the way it has to be. What's the reason? Is it cultural, physiological, or psychological? Why can't I still keep Jonathan close by as my best friend?"

I didn't respond to Christina's question right away. I was busy observing her. Unlike Adams's other women, Christina's attributes didn't rise from her potential, or her hidden assets. Her qualities were apparent and easily on display: the way she dressed, how she spoke, her accomplishments. Christina Peterson had cast a spell over me.

I finally answered. "I suppose the reason they say you can't is a bit of all three."

Her eyes were still on Adams. How I had planned this conversation to unfold was fast becoming irrelevant. The subject of Jonathan Adams had started well beyond the point I'd expected we'd finish.

"So I'll have to get used to missing him, won't I?" she said. "I'm upset with him, Tom. I wish he had given me some of the hints that are so apparent now—that I could have been his companion, his lover, the object of his affection. These past four years, I've watched him get involved with carloads of other women. Jonathan seemed so quick to start relationships with them and he moved so slowly to start one with me. What was I supposed to think?"

The cliché about ships passing in the night came to my mind as I listened to Christina talk.

"I'm involved with Richard now. Very involved, I'm afraid. I'm not sure how that happened. But it's all moving too fast for me to jump off without getting hurt and without hurting and deeply disappointing Richard and everybody else we've involved."

I was struck by how similar Christina's reasons

were to Lisa Chandler's. Their rationale was excruciatingly adult and responsible. Otherwise, when Adams mentioned anything about Lisa and Christina, he described two vastly different women. My mind lapsed back to a childhood spent watching too much television. A variation of Spock's Vulcan creed on *Star Trek* pulsed through my brain: "The needs of the many outweigh the needs of the few." The principle ran counterclockwise to thoughts and deeds emblematic of our generation, and of the two that had followed ours. I wondered where this rare perspective came from and how it had embedded itself inside Adams's two most extraordinary women.

"We are what we know," Christina said. "There have been three men in my life, besides Richard and Jonathan: my ex-husband, a Mayo Clinic doctor, and a Minneapolis writer. My husband was my opposite. The doctor was too much like me. The writer brought a truckload of issues along with him and into our relationship—issues that could only be solved by years of therapy. And therapy would probably have killed his talent as a writer." She laughed.

I wondered how Adams would have fit into her pantheon. The more she talked, the more I understood how Hunter had snared her. He was romantic and attentive, while somehow oblivious to anything soft.

"Richard is a fixer," Christina explained. "He makes life easy. I'm hardly responsible for anything. It's like being on vacation. Things have changed so much these past two months," she continued. "It's strange. When I try to figure out what happened, I find myself falling back to Maslow's theory, his hierarchy of needs: food, water, and shelter; safety; belongingness and love; self-actualization. You know it, don't you, Tom?"

I nodded.

"Richard provides me with almost all of those needs. He's as good as anyone has ever been to me. I needed to feel love when Jonathan was in Iraq. I hadn't received a single e-mail from Jonathan for weeks, much less a letter or a phone call. I didn't realize how much I needed to be loved until the first time Richard touched me—the same time he told me he wanted me to be the center of his life. Maybe I should have been concerned. It probably happened too soon after we met—too fast. But what he said and the things he did were so disarming. I was tired of having to fill my emotional needs all by myself. I was drained. It took an inordinate amount of energy to ignore and deny them. I missed the feeling a woman has when a man desires her so much that he can't keep his hands off her; the look in his eyes when he's consumed with passion."

Christina stopped for a second, surprised by her candor. She blushed.

"Jonathan kept me an arm's length away from him. He'd run us right up to the edge, and then he'd stop. When we were intimate it was wonderful. But I often had the feeling he was holding back. I couldn't figure out why. The times I enjoyed most with him were the times when he let down his guard after he drank a little too much." Christina smiled. The look on her face was the same one she had in the picture on her wall of the ferry boat ride on San Francisco Bay.

The smile that curved her upturned lips straightened. Her tan-and-green eyes opened wider. I was flattered that she quickly felt comfortable in my presence—that she was so at ease that she had already shared intimate thoughts with me.

"I was beginning to think I was past my ability to make a man want to take me to bed with him—that I had lost my attraction that way. Richard put that to rest. I hope you don't think I'm superficial, but that's important to women."

The experience she described had surely been a pleasant one for Christina, but her face was drawn and she frowned as she tiptoed around its edges.

"But let's go back to Maslow and Jonathan Adams," she said. "Jonathan has the unique ability to fill my need for self-esteem. He respects me; he listens. He values my opinion. He's even helped me see flashes of self-actualization. He gives that part of himself so easily, so readily; most importantly, so sincerely and so transparently. I expect he shares that quality with all of us who love him. That's the reason we fall in love with him. Richard can't do that. No man I've ever been with can do it like Jonathan does. But I needed to feel security and belongingness, too. Like every human being, according to Maslow, I need those things first."

Falling in love was an elaborate Kabuki dance for Adams. Only he understood and appreciated the intricate moves he had developed and painstakingly refined. His dance was intended to have shown three women that he was in love with them. Like Kabuki, Adams's way of communicating this was a dying art form. The presentation took too long. The moves were so subtle that they went unnoticed.

I decided that evening at Christina's house, at Richard Hunter's party, that love allowed to flourish in full bloom was more dependent on good timing than it was on great chemistry.

I encouraged Christina to talk more. She told me

the same life-story that Adams had shared with me on Thursday night. I pretended like I hadn't heard it before. As I listened, I decided that Christina was a prisoner of her outstanding qualities: honesty, loyalty, maturity, and steadfastness. Her Scandinavian roots—compassionately nurtured, tempered by fairness—produced a compelling need to set and respect boundaries—something as iron inside Christina as it was cheesecloth inside Adams. Richard Hunter's headlong dash into her life had taken her by storm and overwhelmed those boundaries. Hunter had made himself so much a part of her space that getting him out of it would cause monumental upheaval.

But Christina's thoughts as she expressed them that night, her words, their tone, her gestures, suggested the door was still open for Jonathan Adams. But it wouldn't be open long.

"I love Jonathan, Tom. But I can't do anything about it now."

I seized upon the word "now." I bagged it for evidence so it could be dissected and analyzed later. I memorized and replayed the velveteen softness of Christina's voice when she said it.

I had had Christina to myself for a long time. A few guests were starting to leave and a stern look from

Hunter, suddenly standing on the lawn a few feet in front of us, was meant to remind Christina that she had an obligation as cohost to thank them for coming. Our remarkable discussion was abruptly ended.

Christina was gone. Adams was made inaccessible to me by a phalanx of friends and neighbors, so I sought out my new friend, the writer-turned-farmer. We cut ourselves loose from the group. I enjoyed his bag full of stories about his adventures in dairy farming, and his homilies about country life, until his wife came and pulled him away from me with a gentle reminder that he had twenty-five cows that expected to be milked at dawn the next morning.

As Hunter increasingly became the party's center of attention, the closer he drew Christina to him. It was painful for Adams to have to watch. His dwindling flock of friends could distract him from the spectacle no more.

"I think it's time for us to go home, Tom. How about it?" he asked.

I would have left sooner.

After we made our perfunctory good-byes to Hunter and his crowd, I preceded Adams out the door by a full minute. We figured that might afford him a pretense to leave what was left of the party as quickly as possible: "Tom must be outside waiting for me. Better go."

Christina walked us to the end of her driveway. She hugged me and kissed me on the cheek. She whispered how much she enjoyed our talk. Then she turned to Adams and extended her arms, inviting an embrace. They held each other for a long moment. Her hands moved up his back, then along his arms, and finally to the sides of his neck. She gently pulled his face close to hers. Her lips found his mouth. Their kiss lasted long enough to make me feel like a voyeur—an experience Julie Cook's mother had never allowed us the opportunity to enjoy on Byron's Lane.

Christina turned from us and walked up the driveway, toward her lighted house, back to Richard Hunter and her new friends. She never looked back.

I had witnessed a mixed signal that I struggled to interpret. Adams's bewildered look, as he stood frozen at the foot of Christina's driveway, watching the back of her until she disappeared into her house, told me he was struggling, too.

*

Back in Adams's house, the kitchen clock showed half

past twelve. Before we went to bed, we drank a Scotch nightcap on Adams's deck. At his insistence we discussed the details of my publishing company's pending sale to Disney. Adams speculated that taking a tendered position as a senior associate at either the Robert Wood Johnson Foundation or the Brookings Institute, think tanks focused on the national health care crisis and the role of government in a democracy, might be a good way to keep him engaged in public affairs and constructively fill his time after he quit elected politics. Adams looked toward Christina's house. Its bright lights showed through thinning trees.

We didn't talk about Christina. But Maggie and Kathy found a way into our discussion.

Adams rocked back in his chair. He held his drink close to his chest. "I think about Kathy sometimes. But it's getting difficult lately to pull up her face when I close my eyes and think of her. I haven't seen Kathy in twenty years. I'm deeply, deeply bothered that she's fading from my memory."

While he was talking, I shut my eyes. Maggie's face and form were not as sharp in my mind as they used to be, either. I nervously reached in my wallet for her picture. I pulled it out and stared at the photograph in the faint porch light.

Maggie and Kathy had become good friends over

the years. My indivisible friendship with Adams, and Kathy's growing closeness to Maggie, afforded Adams opportunities to have contact with his wife after their divorce. Maggie and I were determined that their separation would not affect our association with either of them. I still get Christmas and birthday cards from Kathy, but when Adams asked me how long it had been since I talked to her, I couldn't precisely remember.

"The last time I saw Kathy was at Maggie's funeral," Adams reminded me. "We met the day after, at Maggie's favorite sidewalk café in Greenwich. Kathy told me that she was still in love with me. She said that seeing me, even infrequently, was becoming too difficult for her. She told me that she had met someone back in Oregon and that they planned to get married that Christmas." Adams stirred his drink with his finger and stared into the top of his glass.

"I remember Kathy saying that the guy she would marry 'was no Jonathan Adams.'" He laughed. "She tried to explain to me how that was a curse and a blessing. Then she got up from the table, kissed me on the forehead, insisted on leaving five dollars for her coffee, and walked away." He put his glass to his mouth and took a drink. "I've never seen or heard from her since."

After pausing, Adams continued. "I had two affairs

when we were married. They were back-to-back. One was with an undergraduate student; the other was with my thesis advisor. I killed what was left of Kathy and me," he confessed. "I had no desire to get involved with either of those two women. They both pursued me. But I made it easy for them. Maplewood cursed me with an oversized need to be loved and admired. Both women pushed those buttons. For a few weeks I was someone special in an unprecedented way in someone's life. The price I paid to feel that was god-awfully high. I crave that feeling. It's addictive. I'm not sure I wouldn't do it again—even knowing what it cost me."

For a long time, we sat in silence on the deck. When Adams could no longer see lights at Christina's house shining through the trees, he stopped drinking and went to bed.

*

Showered and shaved by eight in the morning, I was tugged downstairs to the kitchen by the smell of bacon and cinnamon buns. On my way by the bedroom mirror I checked to be sure the buttons on the collar of my denim shirt were fastened. There was surely company downstairs—someone who had happened by after I went to bed or early that morning—making Adams breakfast. He'd cooked oatmeal for me once, and sprinkled it with brown sugar and raisins. But every other breakfast I'd shared with him at his house was either dry cereal or served by one of his women.

I stood in the entry from the hallway to the kitchen, enjoying a sight as rare as the aurora borealis and almost as impressive.

The Sunday newspaper was spread over the tile-topped work counter. Four barstools were arranged around two sides of it. Adams was in an unfamiliar pose, bent over the stovetop, spatula in hand, dabbing at scrambled eggs cooking in a black iron skillet. As soon as he saw me, he picked up an empty plate. Before he handed it to me, he used it to point at a small mound of bacon strips and a pastry-filled cookie sheet, just out of the oven. It was my signal to fill half the plate and bring it back to him to fill the rest of it with his scrambled eggs peppered with fresh mushrooms.

"There's milk and orange juice in the refrigerator. If you want coffee, you'll have to make it yourself. Glasses and coffee mugs are in the cupboard next to the sink. While you're up, would you get me some juice?"

In a few minutes we were sitting on barstools,

opposite each other, busily devouring the newspaper and the food on our plates. Breakfast and a Sunday morning newspaper stifle conversation, especially among men. It always happens that way, even when good friends are only a few hours away from taking leave of each other. After a long silence, without looking up from the paper, Adams voiced a grunt of disgust.

He was reading a guest editorial written by a first-term Republican senator from Florida who was asserting that any president of the United States not fully supporting the junior senator's version of what U.S. foreign policy should be was spineless and wrongheaded. Adams read parts of the editorial out loud to me. He wearily shook his head. "We're six percent of the world's population and arrogant enough to truly believe that our hopes and fears ought to be everybody in the world's hopes and fears. Most people don't think like we do. And damn few share our priorities."

A grin came across my face. Adams had just translated the gibberish of our dysfunctional global society into a short, coherent observation. This from a man who didn't know how to analyze, diagram, or explain the meaning of the simple sentence: "This is who I am."

"Priorities imply choices, Tom," he continued.

"And most people in the world don't have the luxury of being able to make choices. They don't have alternatives. That's not just because their leaders prohibit them; their standard of living doesn't make choices available. Our freedom of choice is what makes people want to live and work in the United States."

I enjoyed listening to Adams talk passionately about things he believed in. I'd missed that for most of the past four days. Maybe that edge of him was starting to come back. I put down my part of the newspaper and gave him all of my attention.

"We Americans don't realize that planning ahead and making choices has never been a regular part of most people's day," he continued. "Most of our politicians don't have a clue that the rest of the world is wired to think differently than us."

I looked at Adams, his eyes intently focused on the opinions section of the newspaper. He picked it up off the counter, bringing it closer to his face.

I tried to temper his remarks and provide some perspective. "Maybe it is better said that we Americans are programmed differently than the rest of the world."

I made my comment in a purposely off-handed way, making the point that his words betrayed traces of arrogance lingering in his American soul, too.

"There are almost twenty-five of those differently

wired people for every one of us," I reminded him.

Adams pulled his face up from the newspaper and smiled at me. Then he buried his head in the newspaper again.

"Choices." He said the word in a hard way, and paused for a second. "God, we've always had more than enough choices, haven't we? I hate having to make them. They make me too deliberate. I need to project energy."

"I beg to differ," I replied. "It's an honest matter of opinion about which does more damage to the human spirit—a lack of vitamins, or the complete surrender of choice."

Adams laid the newspaper down on the kitchen counter and stared at me. "Is that an original thought?" he asked.

"What do you think? Is it black-book worthy?"

"It certainly is," he said.

"Then I had better footnote it. I read it in a manuscript I edited last month. The book's about Harry Hopkins, the New Dealer who ran welfare programs for Roosevelt during the Depression and was his confidante during World War Two. Hopkins said it, but I've often thought it."

Adams laughed as he opened a drawer beneath the

countertop and pulled out a pen. He wrote my quote on a paper napkin.

*

Two hours later, Adams drove me to the airport. When we passed Christina's driveway, Hunter was at the end of it, collecting her newspaper from a green tube next to her mailbox. He waved. We courteously smiled back at him. The likelihood that within the next five minutes Christina would be lounging on her sofa, her feet in his lap, sharing the Sunday *Star Tribune* while sipping coffee he had made for them, destroyed any prospect of Adams's involvement in a meaningful conversation for the next half hour. I spent the entire trip to the airport filibustering.

"Figure out if you're in love with Christina. If you are, or if you're trending that way, make a point to get together with her soon and tell her."

I managed to phrase my message three different ways before we reached the airport.

I didn't think it was my place to share details of the conversation I had had with Christina the night before. If she wanted Adams to hear what she'd said to me, her thoughts were best expressed by her, directly to him. All

I said to Adams was: "I think her door is still open a crack. You need to get your foot in—quickly, before it's closed."

Adams offered no response.

"I wrote down a couple of phone numbers on the back of one of my business cards where you can reach me in California this week if you need some bucking up. I left the card on your kitchen counter. You really ought to have a heart-to-heart with Christina sometime this week."

The trip to the airport was the first time Adams had driven me anywhere while not exceeding the speed limit. When he dropped me curbside, in front of the door that opened to my airline's ticket counter, he finally spoke.

"What you said has some merit. Maybe it's time for me to learn how to do things a different way. I've got to shake this Iraq thing and get focused on something again."

The possibility of his careful consideration of my argument, given his dismissal of it just days before, gave me reason to hope that he was about to make a serious attempt to deal with his corrosive, debilitating fear of rejection.

"It looks like I'll have no plans for Thanksgiving this year. Let's get together in New York," Adams said as I pulled my bag from the backseat of his car. I told him that that sounded like a fine idea. But I wished hard for a call from Adams in mid-November asking to be excused from the commitment because he had made other plans—with Christina.

"I'll let you know if Breech calls about that Florida golf vacation," he added.

We shook hands in his front seat and said good-bye.

As I stepped to the curb and looked behind me, I noticed that Adams had left his car. When he got to where I was standing, he put his arms around me in a splendidly awkward and meaningful way. No words were spoken. He turned and walked back to his car.

As I took my first steps toward the ticket counters, Adams rolled down his passenger-side window and called my name. I turned around. He was stretched out over the Porsche's front seat, his head almost outside the window.

"Hey, Tom—I'm awfully glad you came."

CHAPTER
FOURTEEN

We had just finished a Thursday morning meeting at Disney when one of the office assistants tapped me on the shoulder and told me I had a telephone call from Minnesota. I looked at my watch; it was one-thirty there. As I walked toward the nearest conference room with a telephone, I was grinning. Two people who passed me in the hallway returned my smile. Adams caused it, not them. But I was happy they misinterpreted it. I wanted to keep its source all for myself.

I was impressed that my friend had pursued my suggestion so soon after I had made it. I was happy things went well; I was sure they had. What I had advised Adams to do smashed against more than forty years of carefully honed tendencies. But what Christina had told me on Saturday night persuaded me that there would be hope in Adams's voice that Thursday. I made a mental note to ask Adams about his Monday meeting with the FBI and the state police. I'd been tied up in non-stop negotiations about the publishing house's sale since Monday morning. I intended to call Adams as soon as they were finished, if he hadn't called me first.

I should have been surprised that he didn't call me on my cell phone or at the hotel. But I gave it no thought as I picked up the telephone receiver.

I pressed the red blinking hold light and started the conversation: "Afternoon, Adams. What's up?" But the voice on the other end wasn't him. As I listened to the person who had called, my left hand holding the receiver began to shake. It shook so much that I felt it bouncing against my ear. My mouth went dry. The muscles in my face collapsed.

Jonathan Adams was dead.

A man who said his name was Sheriff John Michaels asked if it was possible for me to return to Minneapolis within the next day or two. He said he was in the beginning stages of a murder investigation. Because I had been with Adams much of the time between the Monday night shooting and his murder ten days later, he thought I might be able to help them determine what happened and identify suspects and a motive for the killing.

His voice was cold and dispassionate; it offered no sensitivity or compassion. I instantly disliked Sheriff Michaels.

"Murder investigation?" I asked. Emotion had drained from me, flushed out by shock. The strength in my legs deserted me. I fell into a chair next to the desk on which the telephone sat.

"Oh, I'm sorry, Mr. Walker. I've gotten ahead of myself. As you can probably understand, it's a little hectic here today. The FBI is all over the place and I'm trying to clear up all the confusion they're causing."

There was a twinge of excitement in the way he talked. My dislike of Sheriff Michaels grew.

He explained that early that morning, the woman who came to Adams's house every other Thursday to clean it had found his front door slightly opened. She thought it odd. When she pushed the door open further, it bumped against his body lying face up in the hallway. Michaels said that Adams's next-door neighbor, Christina Peterson, to whose house the cleaning lady had run for help, had told him that I should be the first to know about what had happened. My business card with my California phone numbers written on the back of it was found on the kitchen countertop by one of Michaels's deputies.

"I'll be on the next plane," I told him without hesitation. "I'll try to be at your office early this evening."

I got Christina's telephone number from directory assistance. I called her, and the phone rang for a long time. No one picked up and her answering machine didn't engage.

I stumbled back to the meeting and reported the news I had just received; I would have to postpone the rest of our negotiations that week. I had to return to Minneapolis as soon as possible.

I accepted a generous offer from Disney to fly me back on one of their corporate jets.

*

Disney's plane returned me to Minnesota in the same amount of time as the drive from Pine Lake Lodge to Adams's house five days before. I used part of my time in flight to make a list of what had to be done when someone dies unexpectedly: call Adams's sisters, find his will, secure his house and his personal things. I numbly fell back on what I had learned when Maggie had her accident. I called the sheriff's department from a phone on the plane and made arrangements with the sheriff to be picked up at the airport by a uniformed officer. I spent the rest of the flight thinking about Maggie and Adams and Christina Peterson. I watched barren Nevada and Utah, the snow-capped Rocky Mountains, and the browning Great Plains disappear beneath the sloped wings of my jet. I thought about the violent ends that had come to everyone who had ever lived on Adams's property. I cursed his house.

I was slipping from rationality into a dark, churning whirlpool of senselessness. There was nothing around me that I could grab onto to stop my slide. I worried about how Christina was handling the news. I wished I hadn't told the sheriff that I would head directly to his office when I landed in Minneapolis. I needed to grieve. I knew I could only do that effectively in Christina's company.

Minneapolis was still an hour away. I was having a very hard time comprehending that my best friend, Jonathan Adams, was dead. I struggled mightily, trying to figure out what had happened. My grief turned to anger. I directed all of it on Islam, Muslim fundamentalists, and Iraq. Surely if Adams had never gone to Iraq he wouldn't have been killed.

It was late afternoon when the small jet began its descent in an executive airport in one of Minneapolis's southern suburbs. The red taillights of cars clogging the highways below us indicated the beginning of rush hour. The plane landed smoothly. The pilot quickly steered it next to a row of hangars. I wrote out Christina's telephone number on my list as we pulled to a stop. The co-pilot emerged from the cockpit and opened the jet's door. I gathered my things. I tried to pull myself together. I tucked my list into my suit-coat pocket, grabbed my carry-on bag, and descended the six steps on the plane's stairway to the tarmac.

The deputy waiting for me at the airport appeared to be in his late twenties, early thirties. He was a bit heavier than police officers ought to be. He was Hollywood's notion of what sheriff department deputies look like if they work in rural counties, like the place where Adams lived. The officer had driven his police car onto the tarmac and had parked it close to where the plane had stopped. He was half-leaning against his car when I approached him, startling him in spite of my having been in his line of sight for ten yards. The deputy clumsily moved a Styrofoam coffee cup from his right hand to his left and shook my hand.

He introduced himself as Todd Walker. He pointed to a black plastic nameplate above the breast pocket on his uniform that confirmed what he said. He told me that he'd been on the force for two years. To his disappointment, by the time I was seated next to him in his police car, we had already determined that we shared no relatives, in spite of our same last name. Then, breathlessly, he started to tell me that Jonathan Adams was his first murder case.

As quickly as he spoke, he stopped and caught himself. Sensing that I didn't share his professional enthusiasm, the deputy profusely apologized to me and offered his condolences. I accepted his apology and took an instant liking to him. Unlike his boss, the sheriff, there was sincerity and empathy in his voice, backed by a look on his face that matched what he said.

I used my cell phone to call Christina's house. There was still no answer.

It was obvious that Deputy Walker wanted to atone for his insensitivity. He did so during our drive to the sheriff's office, by telling me more than he should have about the murder investigation. I desperately needed to know everything I could about what had happened to Adams. Whatever I could find out about his killer and the motive would provide me that smallest measure of understanding I had to have to help break my emotional free fall. I encouraged the deputy to talk.

A woman—not a man—had been picked up two miles west of Adams's house early that afternoon. When police discovered her, she was seated against a tree on a riverbank, listening to Fleetwood Mac's *Rumors* album on an iPhone. They found her by following a trail she had made through the long prairie grass behind Adams's house. A police dog helped, tracking her path through the woods at the end of the field. Deputy Walker said that the woman offered no resistance when they took her into custody.

Fingerprints on a handgun found in the shrubbery next to Adams's front door matched the woman's fingerprints. As far as Deputy Walker knew, she had not yet confessed to committing the crime. The sheriff was sure she hadn't acted alone. She was from out of town. Since last Monday afternoon, she had been staying at the Budget Inn Motel. I kept what I knew to myself.

My friend's alleged killer was registered as Mary Rose Fillmore. She had no criminal record. She drove a late-model Honda Civic with Indiana license plates.

The FBI was convinced that she was a minor player in a terrorist cell. They figured she was set up to take the fall for the terrorists who had planned the murder. The FBI was in the process of rounding up a dozen suspects in the region who were on their terrorist watch list. They called in for questioning all the leaders of the Somali community.

We traveled onto and quickly off an interstate highway that bounded the south side of metropolitan Minneapolis-Saint Paul. The road narrowed to two lanes. Mailboxes along it guarded long driveways that disappeared into seas of trees. Most of the cars we passed had headlights on—dusk was upon us and night was fast approaching. We entered Brookfield on its main street, Sibley Avenue, exactly opposite the direction into town that Adams and I took when we went looking for Linda McArthur the previous Saturday afternoon.

Large parts of the countryside were being swallowed by Minneapolis's sprawling growth, but Brookfield had managed to retain the distinctive characteristics of Norman Rockwell's notion of what small-town America should look like: a vital downtown built around a town square full of stately oak trees; a large gray sandstone courthouse dominating the square; cars parked in neat angled rows on both sides of the streets;

people in business and casual dress standing around and sitting on benches, chatting in the park that filled the square; storefronts and small offices with names stenciled on their windows and doors; folks walking on the sidewalk, crossing the street, going busily about their business before everything would close for the day. They all stopped what they were doing and stared at the police car when we made our fast, noisy entrance into the central business district. The only things out of place in this snapshot of Americana were the four television vans taking up all the parking spaces in front of the courthouse, satellite dishes on each of them pointed toward heaven.

*

Sheriff Michaels had just finished a press briefing. He was in full uniform, reporting the event to a woman dressed smartly in a dark-gray pinstriped business suit, well-fitted and nicely worn over a white silk blouse. He was describing the press conference to her play by play, as if it had been a football game. His excited voice indicated that he was pleasantly surprised at his performance. His demeanor reinforced my negative opinion. I didn't like the man. He was fast becoming a target at which I could misdirect my anger and frustration about what had happened to my friend.

I had been standing in the room for almost a minute before Michaels noticed that Deputy Walker and I were there.

"I'm sorry, Mr. Walker. Please come in. Thanks for picking Mr. Walker up at the airport, Todd. That's all now. You can stand down."

I nodded a thank-you to the deputy before I turned in the sheriff's direction.

"Mr. Walker, this is our district attorney, Marcie Saunders." I shook hands with the sheriff and the woman in the silk blouse. Saunders excused herself. As she left, she reminded Michaels to stop by her office upstairs before he went home.

"Thanks for coming back to Minnesota on such short notice, Mr. Walker. I'm really sorry about your friend. Jonathan Adams was an important, respected, and well-liked person in this state. He'll be missed."

That's everything Adams ever wanted to be, I thought—well-liked, appreciated, and missed. From Adams's point of view, those words would have made a fine epitaph. But they were too personal to be offered by a man who hardly knew him. I questioned their sincerity, although Adams never would have. He would have taken the comment at its face value and quietly reveled in it.

"Mr. Walker, let me bring you up-to-date about what happened and where we are now in the investigation. Because it's an open investigation, I can't tell you everything, of course. But I'll tell you as much as I can. The FBI is getting increasingly involved in this. You'll have to find out from them what they know."

I stopped Michaels short. "Thanks, Sheriff. But Deputy Walker briefed me on the way in. May I see the suspect—this Mary Rose Fillmore?"

The scathing look the sheriff shot in the deputy's direction transformed Todd Walker's friendly face into an expression of extreme apprehension. Then the sheriff turned toward me. In the process, he changed his scowl into a politician's smile.

"A civilian interviewing the prime suspect in a murder case is something we don't allow in a criminal investigation, Mr. Walker. I don't—"

I interrupted him again. "I think I know who she is."

At first the sheriff looked startled. But, as I hoped would happen, he quickly saw an opportunity to move his investigation in front of the FBI's. His female suspect had refused to talk to his detectives and the FBI

agents who had tried to interrogate her. She might talk
to someone she knew. He could be miles ahead of the
FBI by the time they arrived at his office in the morning.

A few minutes later, another one of Michaels's
deputies ushered me to a room off a hall that connected
the jail with the sheriff's office. Having seen dozens of
movies set in police stations, I expected the place to be
windowless and sparsely furnished with a metal table,
two or three straight-backed chairs, a two-way mirror
filling one of its walls. But the room looked more like the
sheriff department's break room. It was brightly lit and
sterile-looking, with a coffee maker and a microwave on
a counter built against one of its walls. A water cooler
and two vending machines occupied space on either side
of the counter. In front of the room, nearest the door,
were a sturdy-looking conference table and two squat
oak bookcases filled with law enforcement manuals.
A sloppy circle of brown folding chairs were scattered
about, and the scuffed gray tile floor made the whole
place seem perpetually cold.

I was temporarily left there alone while the deputy
went off to collect Mary Rose Fillmore. I fetched a
folding chair, pulled it up to the conference table and
uncomfortably dropped myself onto its cold metal seat.
I extended my arms out over the old oak table in front

of me and watched the fingers on my hands shake. I couldn't make them stop. Everything around, about, and inside of me was out of control.

The deputy returned a few minutes later with Fillmore in tow. She looked at me straightaway, giving no notice to anything else in the room. Her puffy face blushed, and then erupted into an ear-to-ear grin that turned her expression from astonishment into glib satisfaction. "Well, what do you know? The gang's all here. How are you doing, Tom?"

My knees were suddenly weak as I tried to stand. My mouth was open wider than it should have been. I had lied to the sheriff about knowing this woman. I'd lied to him because I wanted a chance to confront my friend's killer so I could learn more about the conspiracy to assassinate Jonathan Adams.

Pulling the handcuffed woman along with him, the police officer retrieved a folding chair for her to sit on and dragged it to the other side of the table. As the jailer handcuffed Fillmore's wrist to the top of one of the table's legs and released his hold on her, my mind raced, trying desperately to associate the name Mary Rose Fillmore with a person from my past. Her frozen smile and cold stare easily deflected my darting eyes as I searched her face for clues.

Before leaving us, the jailer announced he'd be just outside if I needed anything. He said I could let him know when he looked into the room through the window on the door, which he announced to both of us that he would do every minute or two. He told me to knock on the door or signal him when I was finished. Then he turned and walked out of the room, into the hallway, closing the door behind him.

I was suddenly alone with a woman who knew who I was, but who was a mystery to me. I was experiencing my first tsunami of gut-wrenching emotions that would batter me the next half hour as I struggled to catch my breath and keep my head above everything happening around me.

Mary Rose Fillmore, if that was really her name, looked older than me. She was dressed in faded blue jeans, white socks, and muddy black tennis shoes. An oversized gray sweatshirt that had GAP written on it in big black letters, worn sloppily over a bigger white T-shirt that spilled out the bottom of the sweatshirt, suggested she was overweight. Her short brown-and-reddish hair, gray streaked, needed combing. Black-framed eyeglasses dominated her face. They were the same outdated style frequently featured in the high school yearbook I had found in Adams's bookcase.

The only thing I knew about this person was that it was she who had repeatedly called Adams's house. Engulfed in anger and profound remorse, I wished to God that Adams had answered one of her telephone calls, signaling that he was home, on Thursday. I would have been there when she rang the front doorbell. Adams would still be alive. Maybe I could have prevented the whole thing from happening. My thoughts fast-forwarded to the shooting incident the Monday before. She surely knew who had done that, too. I was certain of these two things, but nothing else.

"You don't recognize me, do you, Tom?" She paused. "Neither did Jonathan."

Her expression turned from an unsavory smile to a combination of hate and disappointment.

"When you were supposed to know me—when you never acknowledged me, even once—I was Mary Rose Vukovich. For three years in high school my locker was next to yours. Here's the giveaway, Tom. Here's the big clue. When we were sophomores, I drove the drivers' education car into the school building. Jonathan's macho basketball coach was afraid to ride with me the rest of the semester. They had to hire somebody else to teach me how to drive."

I didn't need to be reminded about the day the

drivers' education car crashed into the mechanical drawing and wood shop. I knew who she was when she said that her family name was Vukovich. I was dazed and confused. I tried with all my might to keep my feelings and emotions pushed inside. I sought in vain to determine a motive for Adams's murder that could somehow involve Mary Rose Vukovich.

Mary Rose was a rare breed in Maplewood. She was a native. Her father operated a Sunoco gas station in the middle of town when we moved there. He kept the gas station open longer than he should have by fixing old cars in its two cramped service bays. I never saw anyone buy gas at the place. I remember stopping there once to put air in my bicycle tires. After I was finished, her father made me pay a dime for using his air pump. I was afraid of what he would have done to me if I hadn't had fifty cents' worth of change in my pocket. He was a mean-looking, intimidating man.

As the space around the dilapidating gas station slowly filled up with cars her father couldn't fix or sell, a newly incorporated Maplewood city council persuaded the Sun Oil Company to raze the building in which he worked. It had become an eyesore. The council decided that the property was better suited to be a parking lot for the Methodist church and funeral home that bracketed

Sam Vukovich's struggling business. Sun Oil built a new, shiny, white-tile and blue- and gold-trimmed service station half a mile away. Mary Rose's father was left without a job and the responsibility to remove fifteen junk cars from the property in thirty days. He faced a thousand-dollar fine if he didn't remove the vehicles. When he refused to pay, he did jail time.

Mary Rose Vukovich's father ended up working at Maplewood Lanes, a bowling alley that sprang forth from fill dirt piled behind the shopping center. He cleaned and distributed multi-colored bowling shoes that had their sizes marked in large numbers on the backs of them. He fixed the pin-spotting machines when they broke. Once in a while, he helped tend the bar.

For reasons I was never able to understand, but never protested, Maplewood natives—kids like Mary Rose, whose unfortunate accident was to not have been born somewhere else—were ostracized from the cliques that formed and reformed, like mud puddles in May, among our school's burgeoning student body. Our sheer numbers, and the housing developments in which we lived, had overrun them, their families, and the places where they worked—businesses that proudly bore their names, small commercial enterprises that had operated with modest success for many years before we descended upon them. Franchise stores and fast-food chains closely followed us into Maplewood, quickly and ruthlessly driving their struggling shops and restaurants out of business. The experience caused bitterness among almost all the adults in Maplewood who listed the town as their place of birth. Parents often passed their vitriol on to their children.

But Mary Rose Vukovich was undeterred by the legions of us who constantly rebuffed her. Where Adams loathed rejection, Mary Rose was energized by it. She was always trying to fit in somewhere, anywhere, wanting to befriend someone, anyone. The frequency with which she was ignored drove the intensity of her effort. All the focus of her attention had to do was acknowledge any one of a hundred gestures of friendship she made. No one did.

Our meeting in the basement of a courthouse in Minnesota was the first time I'd ever paid attention to her. By the end of our session I realized her relentless, painful quest for acceptance had been a desperate attempt to be pertinent—not perverse, as we had gossiped about.

Mary Rose and I and six of our classmates shared a locker bay in a dark hallway in the bowels of the old high school building, underneath the glaring stares of her forgotten relatives who graduated in senior classes so small that their pictures hanging on the wall were oval portraits of individuals, not hordes of teenagers crowded onto gym bleachers. She'd always try to approach us in the hallway when our paths crossed. When we saw her coming, we'd feign involvement in a deep conversation with the people beside us. When she snuck up behind us, we'd say hello and pretend we were late for an important appointment.

I was violently shaken from all these memories when she dropped another clue, which shed blinding light as to why we were renewing acquaintance at this particular place and time.

"I'm Victor Pavletich's granddaughter. Did you know that?"

She had dropped the weight of heaven and hell on me. My body contorted. I pushed hard against the back of my chair. I was incapable of masking my feelings. The revelation drove rationality up my throat and out my gaping mouth in a silent scream. In some karmic way, I had been an accomplice in my best friend's death.

The farmer's granddaughter stared at her hands calmly folded on the table. She continued coldly and matter-of-factly. "God came to me and showed me where Jonathan Adams—my grandfather's killer—had tried to hide from us." As Mary Rose spoke, I was as close to assuming a fetal position as someone can get sitting upright in a metal folding chair. Her words drifted in and out of my ears.

"Your friend spoke at a convention at the place where I was working in Indianapolis two weeks ago. I recognized him when we passed in the hall. He looked at me, but he never saw me. But I knew who he was. I followed him back here." Her eyes darted about the room as she spoke. They focused on my startled face. "This is the greatest thing I've ever done."

After a few seconds' pause she went on. "My grandparents always talked about how it was the responsibility of every Serbian family to protect each other. Nobody else would. You had to depend on your family. Blood is thicker than water, they said. When someone in your family is harmed, the family has to hit back. No bad act can go unpunished. I've done my duty."

Her words, dripping in my best friend's blood, chilled me. I know she saw me shiver.

Tradition and history—Adams romanticized them. He often lamented their loss among us rootless souls born and raised in America. Tradition and history stalked him from Ohio to Indiana to Minnesota. Tradition and history killed him. I was jolted to my core. Guilt was overtaken by an equally irrational sense that absolutely nothing could ever have been done to stop it.

How did she know that we were in the woods when her grandfather died? Why did Adams have to be the one to pay for what the four of us did—or didn't do? In my shaken state, I was becoming convinced that something much bigger than me had brought this down upon Adams. I couldn't lie to this woman and tell her that we hadn't been there that day. Lying wouldn't bring Jonathan Adams back from the dead. I was small and insignificant, bobbing helplessly in an ocean of karma that had already drowned him.

Mary Rose felt no guilt for what she had done. She hadn't exactly told me yet, in so many words, that she had killed Adams. That indicated to me the inconsequence of the act in her twisted mind. For Mary Rose, the most important aspect of what she had wrought was that she had done what her family and her traditions expected of her. Somewhere in heaven they were looking down at her, smiling and nodding approvingly. In the process, she also laid claim to her fifteen minutes of fame. She was involved in the assassination of a politician—a famous person. For the first time in her life people would be paying attention to her. Whatever happened from that point was of no real concern to her. Her life had been a steady, persistent ache since we moved to Maplewood. The pain was gone now.

As she continued to talk, my questions began to be answered.

Mary Rose told me that everyone touched by Victor Pavletich's death, including the police, knew the day he died that Adams, Wright, Kearney, and I had witnessed his heart attack and done nothing to help save him. She and her family were sure that we had caused it. Margaret Fillmore, her future and former mother-in-law, lived on Shelley Drive and had seen the four of us run out of the woods that day, an hour before Mary Rose's grandmother found her husband unconscious at the edge of his cornfield.

At the family's insistence, a police officer was assigned to follow up on Margaret Fillmore's report. The Maplewood Police Department's first and last stop was Greg Kearney's house. His father, the mayor, persuaded the officer and police chief who knocked on his door that it was impossible to prove that his son and his friends caused the old man's heart attack. At worst, we were guilty of trespassing and not being good Samaritans. If the Pavletich family wanted to pursue it, Kearney's father was prepared to ask tough questions in a very public way about whether protecting property from juvenile trespassers justified shooting a shotgun at them. These were All-American boys doing what all American boys our age do. The man was eighty-three years old and had died of natural causes.

Mary Rose presumed that Jonathan Adams was the one most responsible for her grandfather's death. Her grandfather wouldn't have had his heart attack if we hadn't surprised him Even if he did, he wouldn't have died if we had helped him. She figured it was Adams who told us to run away. After all, he was a leader. Everything Adams did and accomplished before and since showed that leadership was his most prominent characteristic. So he was responsible. "Everybody in high school knew that when something had to be done, Jonathan Adams was always in the middle of it," she said.

She stopped talking and yanked at the handcuffs that bound her to her seat. The act confirmed that the lock on the cuffs had engaged itself. She quickly lost her expression of defiance. She was enjoying her dominance of our conversation. "I guess I took your breath away."

I had had all I could take that interminable day. I caught the deputy's eye as he glanced in the small window in the room's only door; he'd looked in when he heard the table scrape against the tile floor. I told Mary Rose that I wanted to talk to her more the next day. I asked her if I could. Her dead eyes showed signs of life. She finally had a date with a Maplewood High classmate.

"Of course you can, Tom. I look forward to it. I'm not going anyplace. I'll be here." She laughed at her joke as the deputy un-cuffed her from the table, turned her around, and led her back to her jail cell. I didn't react to her laugh. She looked over her shoulder at me as they disappeared through the doorway.

Alone in the room, I held my arms out over the table.

My hands were still shaking.

*

I briefed the sheriff and a state police detective about most of my conversation with Mary Rose Fillmore. I told them about her connection to Jonathan Adams. I made no reference to her grandfather, and I didn't share my suspicion that she acted alone. I mentioned how close she came to a confession. I wanted a second meeting with her—I had more questions to ask. I figured the possibility of me coaxing a confession from

Mary Rose would guarantee me one.

When I finished the briefing I called Christina Peterson again. No answer. I needed to see her. Deputy Walker drove me to her house.

It was a very different place than it had been when I was last there—dark and uncomfortably quiet. No one came when I knocked repeatedly and loudly on Christina's front door and rang her bell.

When we passed Adams's house next door, lights inside and outside were on. Two police cars were parked near his detached garage. Yellow tape had been tacked to the two pillars on his front porch and blocked the entrance into his house.

Admirers, friends, and neighbors had built a makeshift memorial near his mailbox at the foot of his driveway. A mound of flowers was rising from the grass. A small jam of cars had formed on the narrow county road, and a dozen people were busy staring up the driveway at Adams's hexed house. Others were adding flowers, pictures, stuffed animals, and handwritten notes to the growing pile at the end of his driveway. The scene deeply impressed me. Adams would have been shocked at all this. He never was able to appreciate his impact on people and how extraordinarily well he did his job.

When we returned to the sheriff's office around

half past eight, Todd Walker gave me a number to call where I might reach Richard Hunter. I was sure he would know where Christina was. A woman from his answering service said Hunter was out of town for a few days and couldn't be contacted. I assumed he had left with Christina. A call to her dress shop, open late that Thursday night, confirmed my suspicion. I left my number with the woman who answered the phone. It was Christina's responsibility to contact me now.

At first I was bothered that she hadn't made herself available to grieve with me and help me handle the responsibilities for which she had volunteered me to the sheriff. But disappointment quickly gave way to empathy. I knew who Christina was now. As I thought about the tragedy with which we were both trying to cope, I grew sure that her absence shouted her love for Jonathan Adams. If only her sweet, soft voice could have whispered it in his ear that summer, maybe he never would have been alone in his house.

Large parts of me hadn't accepted the fact that Jonathan Adams was gone forever. I was still looking for signs in Christina's actions that told me she was in love with him—evidence that I could joyfully report to my dear friend and tell him "I told you so." Even then, I wanted to make him whole. But the game was over. I was alone in the dark.

I was sitting at an empty desk deep in these thoughts when Deputy Walker tapped me on the shoulder and passed me a note from Sheriff Michaels. The note said he had arranged a car and a hotel room for me for as long as I needed them. I was the only person Mary Rose Vukovich would talk to. That made me important and Michaels potentially famous. The FBI, the state police, and the sheriff's department were mesmerized by the possibility of uncovering a terrorist connection to Adams's murder. As long as authorities pursued it, cable news and the national networks would cover the story.

From the inside pocket of my rumpled blue blazer I pulled the list of things to do I had made on the plane that afternoon. I was anxious to get to my hotel room and finish them. My most immediate task was my most difficult one. I had to tell Adams's sisters what had happened to their older brother. I had to tell them before the story made the morning network news shows. His sisters were all that was left of his immediate family. Although I remembered where two of them lived, I couldn't recall their married names. But I knew that I needed the contact information of just one of them to do what I had to get done—Sharon's.

The first time I saw Sharon was in the shadow of El

Capitan, when I'd first met Adams. She was five years old on the spring day our families came together to view newborn Byron's Lane. Even then, she exhibited all the characteristics of a mother hen. As I watched in amazement, a person smaller than me told everyone it was time to get back in the car. She assigned each of them seats. All of them followed her orders without a whimper of protest. Sharon, living in Houston, was the person with whom I could partner. Whatever she told me to do, I would do. To reach her, I needed Adams's black book. It surely contained her contact information.

I went looking for Deputy Walker again. Then it occurred to me that his shift might be over. Fortunately, I found him sitting on a bench in the police officers' locker room. He had changed from his uniform into a sweatshirt and jeans. Before I could ask, he offered to drive me anywhere I wanted to go.

*

By the time he and I arrived at Adams's house, it was dark inside. The police cars were gone from his driveway. Two young women loitered near the mailbox, tending the pile of flowers. One of Walker's fellow deputies sat in a squad car parked on the road's shoulder. The car's interior dome light shone on the police officer inside. She was using the time assigned to guard the crime scene to finish paperwork. The deputies nodded at each other as Walker turned his car into the driveway and drove us up to the house.

I ducked under the yellow tape barrier across the front porch and used a spare key Adams had given me years ago to unlock the front door. Pushing it open just wide enough to wedge myself in, I flipped on the light switch, an arm's reach away.

One of the switches inside the door turned on the chandelier that hung above the foyer. The other turned on the outside porch light. I switched them both. The front door's threshold was filled with light from the porch. Light from the chandelier bounced off the shiny marble floor and instantly illuminated it. Its light reflected everywhere except where I was about to take my second step.

A large rose-colored circle thinly covered most of the floor area just beyond the reach of the opened door. This was where it had happened. The bloodstain on the marble floor stopped my entry into Adams's house as effectively as if it had been the Great Wall of China. Deputy Walker discretely pushed his way around me as I stood frozen in the open doorway. Once inside, he silently urged me to follow him into the house.

I walked my weak knees into Adams's study and retrieved his black book from exactly the place I assumed it to be—sitting very visibly on the top of his desk.

I passed by the kitchen on my way out. A faint smell of cinnamon lingered there. A half-eaten roll lay on the counter next to the refrigerator. Adams's overnight bag, still unpacked from Saturday morning, had been moved from the foyer to the closest edge of the living room.

I had no desire to be in his house a minute longer than I had to be. But an opened Federal Express envelope and a handwritten letter lying on the kitchen counter caused me to linger there two minutes longer. Deputy Walker watched me stop and pick it up. He told me that the signature slip that had been attached to the envelope was evidence used to help determine the approximate time Adams was shot. It was apparently delivered minutes before Adams answered the door and confronted his killers. Adams was probably reading what was inside the envelope when they rang his doorbell.

I picked up the opened letter next to the empty envelope. It was from Lisa Chandler.

In the first page, she apologized for sending the letter by way of Federal Express. She wrote that regular mail would have been more appropriate for something like this, but she wanted assurance that he had received it, and she wanted it delivered to him as soon as possible. If he was married or living with someone, she wrote, he could say that the FedEx envelope contained business correspondence if asked what was in it. Lisa ended her letter telling him that she had left her husband a month ago. She wondered if it might be possible to meet Adams for lunch sometime soon. She signed the letter "Love Always, LC."

The second page was a poem she had written:

I have played this moment over and over
in my mind

These last two months

Staring at your picture each night

Memorizing all of your features, and every
one of your quirks

Knowing and remembering these things

More clearly than my own

Deep inside, under layers of skin and dust

I know our destiny is written somewhere

Our next page is whispering in my ear
these days

Loud enough to make me smile, too quiet
for anyone else to hear

And I wonder

As I remember your warmth

Your breathing, your touch, your smell

Your life against my own

How I can go forward from here

Without feeling you against my bare skin

My fingers struggle to feel you again

I asked Deputy Walker if I could have Lisa's letter. He said the Fed Ex envelope's only use in the investigation involved the delivery slip; the sheriff's office had taken it. I folded the letter and the poem and put them in my coat pocket. I tried to guess what Adams was thinking in his last moments. He must have had a smile on his face when he opened the door.

As we drove down the driveway, I asked Todd

Walker to stop for a minute at the memorial to Adams that was growing next to his mailbox. I stepped out of his police car and pulled Lisa's letter and her poem from my pocket. I slid them beneath a scanned picture of Adams shaking hands with one of his anonymous admirers that was pinned to a bouquet of daisies. I stood there for what Todd Walker must have thought was a very long time.

We stopped at a liquor store on our way to the hotel, a Holiday Inn on the other side of town. When Deputy Walker dropped me off at the hotel he gave me his card and told me call him if I needed anything. Forty minutes and three drinks later I was sitting on the edge of one of the twin beds in my room, on the telephone, telling Adams's sister, Sharon, very bad news. From a thousand miles away, I felt her crumble.

I ended up handing off the ball to Adams's brother-in-law. We divided what had to be done between the two of us. By two o'clock in the morning all the items on my list were crossed off, or names had been written to identify who was responsible for following up on the matter.

Every bit of energy and emotion had been pressed from me. I had only enough left to pull a bedspread over my fully clothed body. My carry-on bag lay unopened on the unused bed next to mine.

In spite of my exhaustion, Adams's black book kept me awake for a few more minutes. The sacred Cummings poem shared space in the inside pocket with Adams's well-used passport. A neatly written worn page that described locations of important papers and legal documents was the first page in the section where I had written the Lawrence of Arabia quote the Saturday before. About half of the pages in the section were blank. Eight plastic inserts held room enough for forty-eight business cards. All the sleeves were filled. Half the cards belonged to famous people with whom I had no idea Adams had dealings. Cell phone numbers and e-mail addresses were written in ink on several of them.

I had found his sisters' names, addresses, and phone numbers in an alphabetized address book in the Day Runner's mid-section. As I was surveying the names, I began to drift off. I was temporarily shaken awake when a folded blue envelope fell out of the book onto my chest. I recognized it as having come from Adams's office at the university. It was among the mail that had been pushed under his door on Friday.

The envelope contained a piece of plain white stationery on which a message written in newsprint cutouts had been taped. Six words were glued to the paper: "Your time is up. It's payday."

The mystery of the UM threat letter was solved.

*

I awoke at seven the next morning when the telephone on the nightstand next to my bed rang. The opened black book rested face-down on my chest; the letter and the blue envelope lay beside it. It was the hotel clerk calling to tell me a car had been delivered for my use and the keys could be collected at the front desk. I found a pair of slacks and a shirt inside my bag that were slightly less wrinkled than the clothes I had slept in. I showered and shaved, skipped breakfast, and checked in with Sharon in Houston. She told me that she and her two sisters, accompanied by their husbands, would be in Minneapolis late that afternoon, and asked me to reserve rooms for them at my hotel.

My date with Mary Rose Vukovich was at nine o'clock. I called the office in New York to tell them where I was. I barely made it to the courthouse in time.

Sheriff Michaels was in a bad mood when I met him in his office. His confidence and the prospect of celebrity had been replaced by barely concealed anger and frustration as he introduced me to an FBI agent named Hutchinson. When Agent Hutchinson saw me enter the room, he got up from a desk behind Michaels and stood next to him. The sheriff announced that the FBI would be assuming responsibility for the rest of the criminal investigation of the Adams case.

"The Adams case" was a sterile phrase that welled up anger from my numbness. I was an integral part of "the Adams case" but had no investment in any of its process or even its outcome. My only reason for cooperating with authorities was that it allowed me a chance to crawl inside Mary Rose Vukovich's head and find out why Jonathan Adams had to die; it also assuaged the fear that I was in some way responsible. The FBI agent stepped in front of Michaels and extended his hand to me.

Agent Hutchinson was a short man. A lifetime of dealing with his stunted stature caused him to stand oddly straight, making him more imposing than he really was. His face was thin. Its sternly chiseled features were appropriate for a man whose carefully crafted appearance and rehearsed mannerisms suggested that his vocation was also his life's greatest passion. As he introduced himself, he told me that he enjoyed breaking people down and making them say incriminating things about themselves and their friends. His arrogance caused me to feel odd twinges of sympathy for Sheriff

Michaels.

Hutchinson gave me a list of questions he wanted me to ask Mary Rose. His style and technique were apparently not good enough to make her tell him what he wanted to hear. I tuned him out as he reviewed each of his questions with me, while I mentally developed a list of my own.

Mary Rose was a half hour late. She had been formally charged with Jonathan Adams's murder earlier that morning upstairs in circuit court. Her sweatshirt and jeans had been exchanged for a bright orange county-issue jumpsuit that had the initials "D.O.C." stenciled on its back. A weather-beaten, rumpled-suited, middle-aged man anxiously followed her and a jailer into our familiar room. The rumpled man—her court-appointed attorney—was loudly advising her not to talk to me. She was busy pushing him out the door. I stuffed Agent Hutchinson's list of questions deep into the back pocket of my corduroys.

After her interloping lawyer and the jailer had left the room, Mary Rose began our second meeting by thrusting her free hand across the table that separated us, reaching out for mine. I was repelled by the gesture, but didn't pull my hand back when she touched it. I wanted her to feel comfortable in my company.

"Guess what, Tom? This morning I've already had two meetings with my lawyer, a hearing in court that was covered by four television stations, and a telephone call from a brother who hasn't talked to me in eight years." She smiled, relishing the attention being paid to her, unfazed by the reason for it. I didn't share in the celebration of her celebrity. I changed the topic.

"Mary Rose, what have you been doing since we graduated from high school? I'll bet it's an interesting story."

The surface pleasantness of my request concealed its purpose. I wanted to spend only time enough with my friend's murderer to find out what I needed to know and then leave her company forever. She eagerly told her life story, backing it up to the time of her grandfather's death.

When the Pavletich farm was sold and divided up between housing developers and the school district two years after the farmer died, everybody in our neighborhood assumed his family was financially set for life. I remember listening to my mother gossiping with a neighbor on the telephone about it when the *Maplewood Post* reported that the farm had been sold. I recall feeling assured that a financial windfall for the farmer's relatives would eventually dissipate whatever guilt over his death still lingered in the air of four families' houses on Byron's Lane. Having rationalized that some good had come to the farmer's family from the incident, I put that day behind me, out of sight and out of mind, for a long time. But my hopeful assumptions were false.

The farmer had stubbornly retained his farm years after his neighbors had sold theirs to housing developers. His eighty acres became an island of agriculture, forest, and open space in the middle of an ocean of small lot single-family homes. In a move undoubtedly advised in Jonathan Adams's textbook about land use and maximizing local tax revenue generation, Maplewood's city government began assessing the value of Pavletich's property at its "highest and best use"—single-family homes. Overnight, his land was worth hundreds of thousands of dollars. It was similarly assessed for tax purposes. Tax assessments on the Pavletich farm started soon after Byron's Lane was built. Reassessments occurred almost annually. There was no way Pavletich's modest farm could produce enough income to support him and pay his current and back property taxes. Still, he had refused to sell even parts of his land to the real estate speculators who were always calling his house and camping on his doorstep.

Pavletich paid his last property tax bill six years

before his death. By the time his estate was probated, almost two years after he died, penalties, interest, and principal on what the family owed the city, the county, and the school district couldn't possibly be covered by the farm's assessed value. Real estate developers took advantage of the situation and bought most of Pavletich's farm at fire-sale prices. The family gave away almost a quarter of the land to the school district to satisfy back taxes owed and for a promise that an elementary school planned to be built on part of the land would be named after Victor. The school board was persuaded to change its mind when the largest builder of homes in Maplewood offered a hundred thousand dollars for the new school's naming rights. What was to be Pavletich Elementary School was instead named Antonelli Elementary.

On her twenty-first birthday Mary Rose Vukovich married Danny Fillmore, the only child of Margaret Fillmore, the neighborhood instigator of the short-lived police investigation of our involvement in the farmer's death. Danny was two years behind us in school—a mouse of a boy who grew into a rat of a man. By their second wedding anniversary he was serving ten to twenty years in a state penitentiary for killing a friend in a bar fight. Another twenty years were added to his sentence when he was convicted of murdering a fellow inmate. Mary Rose said she would have waited ten years for him, but forty was too much to expect. She divorced Danny Fillmore when she was twenty-six.

Frequent disagreements with family members eventually drove her from her nest in Maplewood. She flew to Indiana. She went to technical college in Indianapolis and learned how to service mainframe computers. Life was good for five or six years—until large mainframes gave way to desktop computers. Instead of adjusting as the technology changed, Mary Rose opted for the glamorous life of traveling around Latin America and Africa, helping keep a dwindling number of her company's dinosaurs alive, for clients who couldn't afford to upgrade their computer capabilities or pay for her work. The company died. She was unemployed for three years. She eventually took a position as a crew supervisor with the Indianapolis Convention Bureau, setting up and taking down furniture at trade fairs, luncheons, and meeting rooms in the convention center.

During that time she married a Turkish man ten years younger than her. The marriage lasted a week longer than it took her new husband to get his green card and a proper work permit. Her Turkish connection mesmerized the FBI and kept them hopelessly looking for al Qaeda's involvement in Adams's murder.

Mary Rose leaned back in her chair and smiled at me.

"If you had been as interested in me when we were in high school as you seem to be now, maybe I wouldn't have killed Jonathan."

Her cold words hung frozen in the space between us.

My astonished reaction to the tone of her statement was shattered when the door to the room crashed open, banging loudly against the wall. She jerked from her chair. I probably did, too. Our heads instinctively turned in the direction of the noise. Agent Hutchinson and two of his minions had burst into the room.

Two steps inside, Hutchinson gathered himself, straightened up, and calmly walked to the end of the table where we sat. He reached under the table and retrieved a listening device. The surprised look on my face likely convinced Mary Rose I had nothing to do with his plan to entrap her. I hoped the effort was a part of his investigation and not its climax. I had edited enough crime novels in my time to recognize an interrogation technique that might not pass a Fifth Amendment test.

But what was to eventually become of Mary Rose

Vukovich and whether or not she thought I was part of a plan that tricked her into confessing that she murdered Jonathan Adams was of no great interest to me. I had all the information I needed to process the circumstances of Adams's death, and to understand the motivation and twisted psyche of his killer. I hadn't the stomach to hear details about the act of killing Jonathan Adams. I didn't want to see the pictures the police took at the crime scene or hear graphic descriptions of his gunshot wounds. I was thankful that Adams's neighbor, Jim Brandt—the farmer-turned-writer I'd met at Christina's party—had identified his body at the county morgue. I couldn't have done so myself.

As a jailer led her out of the room and back to her cell, Mary Rose looked over her shoulder and tried to dig her heels into the tile floor, slowing his effort to pull her out into the hallway. While she struggled with him, she smiled at me. The jailer loosened his grip on her arm. She pushed him and turned halfway toward me before the deputy recovered his hold on her.

"Tom, my lawyer told me this morning that I might be in court again tomorrow. You'll be there, won't you? He says there'll be lots of television coverage." Her voice was eerily calm, given what her body was trying to do. Mary Rose Vukovich was in the hallway and out of sight by the time she finished her sentence.

Agent Hutchinson transferred his attention from his clandestine listening device to me. "You didn't do what I asked you to do," he lectured. "It doesn't matter. We don't need any more of your help. You can go."

I handed him Mary Rose Vukovich's blue envelope containing the death threat letter that I had stuffed in my pocket at the hotel when I left for the courthouse. I was anxious to get about the business of grieving my friend's senseless death.

CHAPTER
FIFTEEN

The next and last time I was in Adams's house was a month after his murder. The memorial next to his mailbox had been abandoned. Left in the wake of the homage and emotion that built it was a pile of broken pinwheels, deflated balloon hearts, weather-beaten political signs, and handwritten notes whose messages rain had made unreadable. The bright rainbow of flowers that graced the top of this makeshift monument had turned the same colors as the leaves fallen from the trees that bracketed the road in front of his house. Dead leaves had blown up against the side of the mound and were in the process of covering it.

Somewhere in the pile was Lisa Chandler's poem.

Adams's sisters and their families had come and gone from Minneapolis by the second week in October. The last warm days of the year left with them. They had arrived at the crest of a spontaneous, sincere, and widespread expression of a great loss, and a celebration of a life well lived. His sisters had a chance to glimpse the significance of a brother they hardly knew.

Adams's last will and testament—surprisingly detailed, predictably outspoken, mildly controversial, and generally misunderstood—ordered that no funeral or public memorial service be held for him. But his constituents, his neighbors, his friends, and his colleagues and students outvoted him. Most people attributed his preference for no public send-off to his modest tendencies, or his carefully crafted propensity for understatement. I knew better. He didn't want the event to turn out like Jay Gatsby's funeral—a party he threw to which no one came.

It all should have been of no concern to Adams. His friends and supporters, with his sisters' blessing and coordination by the governor's office, held a memorial service at Brookfield's public high school on the evening of the second Wednesday after his death. The newspapers and local television stations reported that six thousand people attended. So many people came that the gathering had to be moved from the gymnasium to the football stadium. Like Adams's infectious grin, exceptional weather smiled down on the hastily organized event. A former president of the United States was there—a closer friend of Adams's than I realized—a talented man, like Adams, who shared some of the same demons. Christina Peterson was not. I don't know if Linda McArthur attended. I looked for her, but didn't see her.

Lisa Chandler came. We talked for a half hour after the memorial service. She told me she would have left her husband and married Adams if Adams had asked her. She said he was, and would always be, the love of her life. She never mentioned the letter or the poem she had sent to him the day he died; neither did I.

Kathy sent flowers. Jim Breech came back to attend the memorial service.

Whatever Adams contracted on Byron's Lane and carried with him like terminal cancer the rest of his life had proven benign. Jonathan Adams was a man whose grasp far exceeded what he believed to be the extent of his reach. It turned out Maplewood had not served Adams as badly as he thought. His experiences there forged a canon of values that positively touched thousands of lives in hundreds of small ways.

The torrent of sympathy for Jonathan Adams washed away any sustained interest in digging deeper into Mary Rose Vukovich's motive for killing him. After a terrorist connection was proven unfounded, the reasons for his tragic death were too complicated for the mass media to unravel a possible cause in a two-day news cycle. The public was unknowingly following the advice Adams's father gave him years ago: confessions won't change what happened, they'll just cause problems and confusion; we need to get on with our lives.

During the month I had been away, the leaves on the young maple trees that lined Adams's driveway had turned from fading green to bright red to gold and brown. Almost all of them had fallen. They crunched under my tires as I slowly drove my rental car on the wet black asphalt. I stopped where the sweep of his driveway touched the cobblestone walk that led to his red front door. I turned off the ignition, pushed a button that rolled down my car window, and sat for a few minutes breathing in the cool country air. Dead leaves swirling on the pavement broke extreme silence that otherwise enveloped Adams's cursed property. The sky over his house had produced an all-day chilling rain. Unlike a spring rain that caused plants to grow, a gray-day autumn rain only made everything wet and miserable.

After the memorial service, matters related to Adams's death remained worthy of space on the front page of the Minneapolis *Star Tribune* and Saint Paul *Pioneer Press* for one more week. Copies of these were piled next to his front door. I wondered out loud to the gray sky and swirling leaves why the newspaper carrier insisted that Adams receive his newspaper three weeks after his very public memorial service.

I picked up the rolled-up newspaper that was least wet and most current. Tucked in the lower left-hand corner of the front page was a two-column story that reported that Mary Rose Vukovich had, through her public defender, entered a plea of not guilty by reason of insanity. Her attorney was quoted in the article as saying that even if the judge and the district attorney didn't accept her insanity plea, he thought his client's case had a fair chance of being dismissed because her confession had been secured illegally. The news in the article didn't surprise me. It didn't bother me, either. I had little interest in how the State of Minnesota intended to deal with my friend's murder. My job was to box Adams's personal things and arrange to send them to his sister in Houston. The furniture and all other household items left behind were to be auctioned off as soon as Adams's estate was probated. State and county authorities promised Sharon that they'd fast-track the process as a favor to the family.

In spite of the sincere public show of sympathy the month before and the oft-stated pledge made by important people at his memorial service that Adams's legacy would be remembered and built upon "for years to come," most of his footprints on earth had already vanished from it forever. The only traces left of him were a fellowship for students at the University of Minnesota who were pursuing bachelor and graduate degrees in American history, and an obscure formula bearing his name that showed how property tax revenues related to land use. The Adams Fellowship would be funded by his savings, considerable investment income from a blind trust whose principal was fueled by royalties from his land-use book, and proceeds earned from the sale of his house and its contents. His fellowship was also structured to provide full college scholarships for his nieces and nephews.

According to Adams's will, his silver Porsche was to be given to the last woman with whom he had had a sexual relationship. I presented his Porsche to the attractive senior education major in his political science class who had persuaded Adams to give her three more points on her exam. Her name and telephone number were written in Adams's black book. Tears and a heartfelt expression of grief when I gave her the keys suggested he was at least her mentor. This part of his will makes me grin every time I think of it. I'm sure he included it to make us either smile or wag our fingers at him. He didn't care which, as long as it caused us not to forget him.

Finally, there were supposed to be three envelopes in the top right-hand drawer of his desk in his home office. I had to collect them and make sure they were delivered to the people whose names were written on them.

He wrote in his will that his body was to be cremated and that his ashes were to be tossed "unceremoniously" into the Mississippi River. That quietly happened the day after the coroner finished his required autopsy, three days after Adams's death. As executor of his estate, I was determined to follow his instructions to the letter. Duties like this—helping Adams implement his carefully crafted plans—had been my job since I was seven years old.

As I approached the front door to his house, I imagined that Adams and his ashes were probably well past Saint Louis by now and he'd be flowing into the warm waters of the Gulf of Mexico by Thanksgiving Day.

A realtor had put one of those big gold lockboxes on the front doorknob, making the extra house key Adams had given me useless. My key was supposed to be able to open the back door, too, so I took the long walk around his house, past the untended lilac bush that had overtaken his woodpile, and climbed the steps up to his deck. On the deck floor, next to the doorway, was a large box with a blue-and-white Hansen's label on it. Inside were the shingles Jim Breech had promised Adams he would send.

Before I put the key in the door lock, I turned around for a last look at Adams's prairie. The late October afternoon sun, low in the gray sky, thrust its rays out defiantly from between layers of dark clouds that tried unsuccessfully to smother them. I was now and forever absolutely sure that Adams had bought this house because of what I was seeing from his back deck.

The vista spread before me was exactly the same as one over seven hundred miles and more than forty years removed from it—the one that stretched out in front of us and the rest of our lives when we were seven years old. The sun shone exclusively over an area that could accommodate development of nine blocks of three- and four-bedroom ranch-style houses with no basements.

"You build the garage if you want one, and you finish the inside the way you want. The three-bedrooms are eleven thousand dollars; the four-bedroom homes cost fourteen thousand dollars. Special financing is available for veterans."

It was the dialogue of a commercial that ran incessantly on Cleveland's television and radio stations and drew us all to Maplewood in 1957. My father could mimic it perfectly. He often did, every time he itched to move somewhere else. He talked about moving all the time.

Memories swept over me again. The undertow carried me through the door I had just unlocked and into the kitchen. I dragged Breech's box of shingles inside.

I looked out over his prairie again before I slid the screen door closed and turned my back to it. I stood in the doorway a long time. Byron's Lane had established our parameters, not our boundaries. Adams should have known that. He should have discovered that in bits and pieces scores of mornings standing on his deck drinking coffee, and hundreds of evenings watching the sun set through his two-story living room window.

I took off my blazer, laid it on a kitchen stool, and dropped the car keys on the counter opposite the sink. I wanted to finish what I had to do as quickly as possible. I hadn't shed my discomfort about being in Adams's house after he'd been killed in it. The first thing that I did was sneak around the first floor and turn on all the lights. Then I started putting Adams's personal things in boxes. I moved quickly from room to room. His sisters wanted all his clothes to be given to the Salvation Army. They said the Salvation Army would come and collect the clothes from the dresser drawers and the closets as soon as I called them, which I intended to do the next day. It would be noticed that dress among down-and-out men hard on their luck in Minneapolis and Saint Paul had improved appreciably the first holiday season Adams was not in our midst to help celebrate.

There were no framed photographs of people displayed anywhere in Adams's house, except for the usual pictures on the wall in a politician's office: Adams shaking hands with two presidents, a vice president, three governors, a Peace Corps director, six ambassadors, and a secretary of state. A nearly empty cedar chest hiding in the back of the walk-in closet in his bedroom contained his college and graduate degrees and the associated badges of achievement someone wears at the ceremonies where they're awarded such things. The chest also stored a portfolio of wedding pictures, programs and credentials from presidential inaugurations and political conventions, three baseball World Series, a Masters golf tournament—and his white high school varsity basketball letter, trimmed in Maplewood royal blue.

The ring Adams brought home from Iraq was also in the chest. I took it out and put it on the desk in his office.

Three boxes in the office closet, stacked among ten years of tax records, contained pictures he had taken. As digital photography made film almost obsolete, his interest in photography waned. Almost all of the photos Adams had taken had been tossed into one of the boxes. He talked once about organizing them in some viewer-friendly way, but later decided that the project was pretentious. "Who would ever want to see my pictures?" he wondered out loud when we visited three years ago. "Nobody" was his answer.

There were a few pictures of Kathy and other significant women he'd dated and lived with, mostly standing in front of scenic backgrounds or familiar buildings and monuments. Most of the photographs were of unidentified, anonymous places all over the world—the kinds of places one doesn't see on a guided tour. Many of them were good enough to be framed and exhibited. Some were stark, yet richly beautiful—landscapes lacking any intrusion of people, with the exception of unidentifiable masses unaware that their picture was being taken.

I dug further into the pile and found an unframed eight-by-ten of a woman leaning against a grocery cart, staring at a six-tiered shelf full of boxes of a hundred different brands of breakfast cereal. I recalled what Adams said about choices the last Sunday breakfast we had together. I decided I'd keep it. I moved the photograph to the kitchen, putting it next to my coat so I wouldn't forget it.

I also decided that the rest of us ought to have a chance to see some of Adams's remarkable pictures. As I sorted through them, I formed a plan to publish a book that included the best of them. The project would afford me an opportunity to keep my friend alive for a few more months. If the picture book sold, the money could be used to augment his scholarship fund.

As I was deciding how to take the boxes of pictures back to Connecticut with me, the front doorbell rang. It took two more rings before I could make my way from Adams's office down the hall to answer it.

My hand on the doorknob, I paused, realizing that what I was about to do, at exactly this place, was a replication of Jonathan Adams's last moment alive. I hesitated long enough to take a deep breath. Then I opened the door. The realtor's lockbox bounced when I pulled the door toward me. The unexpected bang was startling.

On the other side of the threshold stood Christina Peterson.

She smiled at first, and then she frowned. Her blond hair was loosely gathered on top of her head, pinned there precariously, looking like it could all easily tumble down with one casual headshake. She wore no make-up; her face was puffy, her eyes red. She was clad in sandals, jeans, and a sweatshirt that advertised a dolphin rescue center in the Florida Keys.

"I saw a car in the driveway. I hoped it was yours. I wanted to see you before you left."

Christina made no mention of where she had been and why she hadn't made any effort to contact me since Adams's death. They were matters instantly unimportant.

After standing too long in the doorway, I reached over the threshold for Christina's hand and gently pulled her across it. She fell through the doorway and into my arms. We held each other for a long time. Our sobs made our bodies shake. Her neck and her hair were wet with my tears. They were the first I had shed since Maggie's death.

"Can I help?" she asked. She spoke so softly I wouldn't have heard her voice if my ears hadn't been two inches from her mouth. Christina gently pushed back from me and took a tissue from the front pocket of her jeans. She wiped the tears from her face with soft dabs. Then her eyes dropped. They caught a faint red stain that remained embedded in the white grout on the foyer's gray marble floor. Her chin shook, she shivered, and her lower lip began to quiver. Both of us needed to get away from this place.

"Of course you can help," I quietly answered. "I've got a few more things to collect in the study. You can help me finish my walkthrough. You can help me carry boxes out to the car." I reached for her chin and gently tipped her head from the floor to focus on my face. She managed a smile and turned to close the door behind her. She put her arm around my waist and maneuvered us around the rose-stained spot on the floor, down the hallway, and into the study.

Legs crossed, we sat on the carpeted floor, at opposite ends of Adams's office. My thoughts were not about what I was supposed to be doing; they were about how nicely Christina would have fit into Adams's mercurial life. I wasn't as sure that a reignited relationship with Lisa Chandler, dropped unexpectedly in his lap in his last moments, would have turned out as well. But it's likely he would have pursued it, given Christina's involvement with Richard Hunter.

There was really not much more to do at his house that evening. Nervously rearranging things we had already packed away, Christina broke our silence. "I wish Jonathan and I could have had a talk like you and I had at my party."

Christina had pulled from a box a framed picture of Adams sitting with Bill Clinton on a sand dune, somewhere on the Outer Banks. Both of them were staring out at the Atlantic Ocean. She carefully examined it, running her fingers around its edges. She looked up at me.

"What makes us fragile and dissatisfied when we have every reason to be confident and content? Why are we so sad and vulnerable in the midst of having so much?" Her words echoed throughout Adams's disheveled house.

I thought about that glorious night on the dock at Pine Lake. "Too many choices, too few tests and measurements of how we're doing," I answered. This was Adams's opinion, but I had seized it and made it my own. He would have approved.

I put the three boxes of Adams's photographs in the trunk of my rental car. Christina had written my address on them. We made sure they were taped tight enough to accompany me back to Connecticut on my plane the next evening as baggage. I had asked Christina to label the boxes so she would be inspired to keep my address somewhere. It worked. When I returned to Adams's office, she was sitting at his desk, writing my address and my telephone number on a piece of stationery she had found in its half-opened top drawer.

While I had been busy in the kitchen labeling boxes that needed to be shipped to Adams's sister, Christina had found and claimed two items: Adams's State Capitol building access pass and a small brass pelican paperweight that he often absentmindedly played with during long conversations she'd had with him in his office. She noticed me watching her from the hallway. With tears in her eyes, she held the identification badge out away from her so I could see it. She had put it around her neck as carefully as if it had been a pearl necklace. "It's the only picture of him that I'll have, except what's been printed on campaign brochures or in newspaper articles I've saved."

I quickly replied: "I'll send you a better picture of him as soon as I'm home. Keep the ring, too. It's yours. It's next to the computer." I had left the ring in a conspicuous place, on the keyboard of his desktop computer, so I wouldn't forget to take it with me when I left.

She hadn't noticed the ring until I called attention to it. She picked it up and examined it for just enough time to express her admiration. She placed it back on the desk. She looked up at me, puzzled. How could I ever think she'd accept something so special and personal; something that either belonged to or was intended for someone else? What authority did I have to give it away?

I told her how the ring had come to the place where I had found it. I told her how Adams scoured the old bazaar in Amman searching for a setting to match the stone he'd found. I told her how much he looked forward to giving it to her when he returned from Iraq. I explained that I intended to give the ring to her if I ever saw her again. It was hers.

Christina pushed her chair back from the desk. Shaking her head, she leaned slightly forward and put her head in her hands. Strands of her hair fell down to her shoulders. She stared at the ring through cloudy, tear-filled eyes. She was afraid to touch it.

I doubted if it would ever find a permanent place on any of her fingers. What I had told her about the green amber ring made it too special to wear in a casual way. The ring's beauty would cause people who noticed her wearing it to ask where she got it. Its story was too personal to share. But in my presence she took it and put the ring on the third finger of her left hand. She looked up at me and managed a smile through a few sobs and a thick curtain of tears.

"I'm happy you have the ring. Jonathan would be ecstatic."

We both looked at each other for a long time, silent.

"There's one more item of business I have to take care of. Are there some envelopes in the top right-hand drawer?" I asked her. "Would you pass them to me?"

She opened the drawer. It was empty except for three oversized tan-colored envelopes. She lifted them from the drawer and pushed it shut. She was about to hand them to me when she suddenly pulled them back, having noticed the names written boldly on two of them in black felt pen: *Christina Peterson*, *Tom Walker*.

She stared at the envelopes. Then, hands trembling, she gave me mine and the third one, marked *Kurdistan*.

She placed hers reverently on top of the desk. I opened the Kurdistan envelope first. It contained a cashier's check for two hundred and forty thousand dollars with instructions to deliver the money to the families of his murdered Iraqi staff. On a separate folded sheet tucked inside the envelope were their addresses. I showed the contents of the envelope to Christina and told her their story. I folded the envelope in half and placed it on my lap.

I turned the envelope with my name on it over in my hands, like a child does a birthday present, trying to guess what might be inside.

"Can we open them together? Here and now?" Christina asked.

"It's the only way I'd want to do it," I said. I marveled at the possibility that somehow, some way, Adams was directing the scene in which we were acting.

"You open yours first," she insisted in a choked voice, handing me a letter opener she'd taken from a desktop coffee cup. The sound of the letter opener sawing through the large sealed envelope echoed through the room.

Three things were inside my package. They fell into my open, waiting hand and overflowed onto my lap: a tattered black-and-white glossy picture of our Martin's

Amoco Oil Dodgers baseball team, labeled "Maplewood Little League, 1960 Champions"; an opened FedEx envelope that contained a certificate for four hundred shares of Cleveland Indians stock and a stock transfer form with my name on it, signed by Adams and Gabe Chance, dated the day after I left Minneapolis for California; and an eleven-by-sixteen black-and-white photograph of El Capitan in Yosemite Park, carefully wrapped in white tissue paper, signed in the lower right-hand corner in white ink by Ansel Adams.

Smiling through tears, I handed the letter opener back to Christina. She carefully cut the top edge of her envelope and pulled from it something written in blue ink, in Adams's best handwriting, on a piece of letter-sized expensive linen writing paper. She read it silently. Tears tumbled down her cheeks. Her hands were shaking as she tried to pass the paper to me. Her dazzling green amber ring sparkled as it caught beams of light coming from the desk lamp.

It was Cummings's poem, "somewhere i have never travelled." I looked at it. I smiled. I handed it back to her. She carefully put the poem back in the envelope.

I pulled myself up from the floor and took Christina's hand to urge her up from the chair—the same way I had rescued her at her party.

"I know where Adams hides his thirty-year-old Scotch. I'll fetch the bottle and two glasses while you get one of his jackets from the hallway closet and turn off the lights behind us. We'll sit out on the deck and talk about Jonathan and the gifts he gave us."

It was half past ten o'clock—a crisp, moonless late-autumn evening. The sky was clear and cloudless. I had never seen so many stars. It was so dark we could hardly see each other's faces, even though we were sitting just an arm's length apart.